CROSS-FIRE

Cross-fire

GEORGE G. GILMAN

NEW ENGLISH LIBRARY
TIMES MIRROR

For Janet and Roland even though they prefer S.F.

A New English Library Original Publication 1975
© 1975, George G. Gilman

★

FIRST NEL PAPERBACK EDITION DECEMBER 1975

★

NEL Books are published by The New English Library Limited from Barnard's Inn, Holborn, London E.C.1. Made and printed in Great Britain by C. Nicholls & Company Ltd.

450025578

CHAPTER ONE

THE fire burned brightly, the yellow and orange flames feeding hungrily off the clear, crisply cold air of the moonlit night. The man who had lit the fire and cooked himself a meal upon it moved in closer. Squatting on his haunches he turned up the collar of his sheepskin coat, pulled the brim of his hat lower over his forehead and then stretched out his gloved hands towards the heat.

His horse, which was ground-hobbled on the bank of the river thirty feet from the fire, vented a low snort as if registering resentment of the man's comfort. But then, from far off, came the throaty howl of a timber wolf and the tan gelding pricked his ears and forgot about the man.

The camp had been made late – the time was past midnight and a new day was being darkly born – on a site which provided all the basic needs of rider and mount. It was in a wooded gorge cutting through the rugged grandeur of the Uinta Mountains in an area of country where the territories of Utah, Colorado and Wyoming met. The fifty-foot wide river provided sweet water, there was lush grass to feed the gelding, a good supply of kindling from the many stands of spruce, and a degree of weather protection under the towering walls of the gorge.

The wolf did not howl again and the gelding settled. The only sounds within the gorge were the crackling of the burning fire and the rippling of the slow flowing river against the reed-lined banks. The man listened to these for a few moments and felt his eyelids begin to droop. Sleep

5

would be easy to come by tonight and, for a while, he disturbed the peace of the gorge with the noises he made in preparing to bed down.

First he fed fresh kindling to the fire, then spread out his bedroll and took off his boots, coat and hat before sliding under the blankets. He checked that his rifle was within easy reach of his right hand. Then he used the coat as an extra blanket, pulling the sheepskin high up under his jaw, and positioned his hat over his face. Thus his surroundings were lost to his sight. For a while, he continued to hear soporific sounds of fire and river. And, twice, he heard the distant moaning of the wind through the high peaks of the Uintas. Then he slept, as the first crystals of white frost settled on the trees, the grass, the reeds, the coat of the gelding and the covers of the man. Soon, every feature of the gorge save the river and the fire was cloaked in a stiff veneer of sparkling whiteness that reflected the brightness of the near full moon to rob the night of much of its dark.

The heavy frost was like the final brushwork of a great artist, putting the finishing touch to a canvas of immense natural beauty. The gunshot was an obscene defacement.

Adam Steele awoke at once. And his reaction to the familiar sound was instant. He folded up into a sitting position, hat flying off his face as both hands fisted around the Colt Hartford rifle. He half-turned from the waist, to peer towards the distant source of the shot, as his left thumb cocked the hammer of the rifle.

For stretched seconds, the river and the fire were silent. Then the gelding snorted. This time, the sound had a scornful tone and the man treated his horse to a good-humoured grimace.

'Just don't like to take chances, boy,' he murmured. 'Even over a shot in the dark.'

The trace of humour left his face and his expression was earnest again as he stared up river. But there was nothing to see except the moon-silvered water, the spruce and the rock walls of the gorge. The shot had been exploded far beyond his range of vision and there had been no ensuing sounds to offer any explanation of why it had been fired. Then, as he felt the chill of the frosty night bite through his shirt to attack his flesh, Steele shrugged. The shot could have an innocent explanation or it could have been trouble. Whichever, it had nothing to do with him.

He eased the rifle's hammer back to the rest, tossed some more kindling on the fire and warmed himself close to the flames before he bedded down again, adopting the same relaxed posture as before. But sleep was not so easy to come by this time for there was a nagging anxiety in his mind. It hung on the peg of the isolated gunshot and swung like a weighty, finely balanced pendulum, arcing back and forth across his consciousness: its constant movement keeping sleep at bay.

The shot in the night was a symbol of the trouble and violence which had become as much a part of the life of Adam Steele as eating and breathing. Yet, for many weeks now, he had ridden the western territories in easy peace. The .44 calibre revolving rifle had remained silent; the wooden-handled knife had been drawn from the boot sheath only when it was needed for routine chores; the scarf with the weighted corners had served only as a neckerchief; and the pin with the ornate head had stayed resting behind the lapel of his coat.

There had not been a hint of trouble until the gunshot shattered his peaceful sleep. And now, as he lay under the warmth of the covers in the cold gorge, the threat which the distant sound might have offered retreated further with every quiet second that passed. But still sleep was withheld from the man. Trouble was overdue; and, although he felt fully equipped to deal with it, it was none the less an expectation that made for a restless sleeping partner.

7

But then, because Steele was a rational man, he beat the swing of the mental pendulum and, as his mind became settled, he slept. During the remainder of the night, no other external sounds invaded the tranquillity of the high country gorge and it was the frustrated squawking of a flock of hungry gulls which roused Steele a few minutes after sunrise.

He awoke with the memory of the gunshot still ringing in his ears and this fact irritated him. And he continued to frown as he lit a new fire on the dark ashes of the old and set coffee to boil and breakfast to cook. In repose or when he was smiling, Steele's face possessed a kind of nondescript handsomeness. It was a long face with regular features, reflecting his true age – the early thirties: this despite the premature greyness of the once-red hair that he wore at a neat length. A lean face burnished to a dark colouration by weather and beginning to show the first lines to score his advancing years. A face with hard, coal-black eyes, the potential harshness of which was counteracted by his gentle mouthline.

Frowning – as he continued to do while eating the breakfast of bacon, beans and sourdough bread – it was the face of a man who had suffered, its basic form hardened and the time lines deepened. If there had been anybody about to see him, they might well have found themselves provoked into the beginnings of fear by the face of the man.

The sun had risen high enough now in altitude and heat to melt the frost crystals. Steele moved away from the fire and down to the bank of the river. By reflex action – as automatic and involuntary as drawing breath – he picked up the rifle and carried it with him. He stripped off every item of his clothing, raked a narrow-eyed stare across each point of the compass, and plunged into the clear, sparkling water. It would be several hours before the sun warmed

8

the river and its chillness penetrated deep inside him as he stroked himself easily across to the far bank. He did not pause to rest, but made an agile turn and immediately returned to where the rifle lay across the discarded clothing at his starting point.

Still naked, he lifted his gear and went back to the fire. The body he towelled dry with a blanket was neither tall nor broad. He stood a mere half inch above five and a half feet and there was not an ounce of excess flesh to pad his compactly built frame. But there was an obvious strength about him, visible in the hard texture of his skin and the way his muscles rippled close to the surface with each slight movement he made in dressing himself.

Fully clothed, except for the sheepskin top coat, buckskin gloves and wide-brimmed hat, there was an air of a dude gone to seed about Steele. For he wore two-tone boots of black and white, a pale blue city suit, purple vest and white shirt with a frilled collar. Every item was store bought and expensive, but was also stained and ingrained with the grime and dust of long travel. The slit down the outside seam of the right leg of his pants, at calf level, was not however the result of hard wear. It had been there from the day he bought the suit – to enable him to reach through and draw the knife from its boot sheath.

Despite the swim, Steele continued to feel dirty as he undertook the chores of breaking camp. And the three-day growth of beard on his cheeks and jaw was an additional irritation to him. But he was out of soap, and the rattlesnake-spooked gelding had stepped on his razor and snapped it at a former camp. However, it was not a naturally neat and clean man's aversion to being dirty that kept the frown firmly in place on Steele's features. As he packed his bedroll and saddled the gelding, he was still conscious of the gunshot in the night as a symbol of the trouble that must surely attach itself to him soon.

The horse, sensing the unfamiliar mood of concern that gripped the man, eyed Steele balefully after the cinch was tightened – the final act before the day's ride. And Steele, whose Virginian upbringing had given him a deep rapport with horses, rested a gentle hand on the animal's neck and raised a crooked grin to his lips.

'You reckon it's a sign I'm gettin' old boy?' he asked rhetorically. 'Worrying about things before they happen.'

On cue, the horse raised and lowered his head in a deep nod. Then he raised his head again, flared his nostrils and craned his neck around to stare out of wide eyes across the river. The movements were less pronounced than when the rattlesnake had spooked him but the signs were none the less there to see. The animal had been listening calmly to the soothing voice of the man: then something had made him nervous. Steele's hand began to move on the tan coat, stroking the gelding's neck. His free hand was ready to reach for the stock of the Colt Hartford jutting from the saddle-boot: but his eyes explored the potential necessity first – and found the need lacking. The man approaching the riverside camp site posed no threat.

'But he sure looks like trouble,' Steele muttered, his mouthline tightening into a frown once more.

The man was floating in the sun-sparkled water and even from fifty feet away, Steele could tell that he was dead. For he was face down, his head and torso submerged. Just his rump and his legs – the air trapped inside his pants ballooning the denim – kept him partially afloat.

The slightly built Virginian did not move and the gelding, having caught the scent of death but no aftermath of threat, resumed an easy stance. For several moments, it seemed as if the body would float on by, perhaps to go all the way down this backwater until it was emptied out into the Green River tributary of the Colorado. But, abruptly, as if the river spotted the opportunity to be rid of its grisly burden, a cross current took a grip on the corpse and set it on a new course. Once the change of direction had happened, the speed of travel was increased. If the man had been alive and a strong swimmer, he could not have reached the reeds in front of Steele any faster.

The Virginian had already pulled on the skin-taut black gloves: and this not from any feeling of revulsion on touching a corpse. For the gloves served two purposes: one to keep out the cold if the weather dictated; and the other as a kind of good luck charm. And in this instance Steele considered he would be able to use some luck if he chose to pull the corpse out of the river. The gunshot in the night had portended something like this.

The body was thrust by the current into the reeds and the strong-growing tangle held it there – less than a yard from the dusty toecaps of the Virginian's boots. The close proximity of the dead thing triggered the gelding's nervousness again and, free of the rope hobble, the animal side-stepped away. Steele stooped and reached forward. He hooked both gloved hands under the dead man's belt, eased him sideways-on to the bank, and hauled him out of the river. He moved backwards a couple of steps, and rolled the man over on to his back. He stayed in a crouch and the frowning lines of his face did not alter as he looked upon the reason for the man's death.

He had not drowned. A heavy calibre gun – probably a rifle – had been held close to the right side of his head. The bullet that exploded from the muzzle had burrowed across the top of his face, gouging through the back of both his eyes before bursting clear below the left temple. The eyelids were raised, but the eyes were now simply balls of congealed blood. The entry and exit wounds had been washed clean of gore. The lips were drawn wide, revealing the teeth, clenched together in a tight grimace of unbearable agony.

He had been a man of middle years and, judging by the quality of his sodden clothing, certain substance. A balding, clean-shaven, well-dressed man with all his own teeth and an ancient scar on his high forehead. A man who carried nothing in his shirt pockets; some loose change and a handkerchief in the side pockets of his pants; and a billfold in his hip pocket. In the billfold was twenty-five dollars – one ten, two fives and five ones – and a half-dozen pasteboard visiting cards which named the man as Henry Jaggs and proclaimed him manager of the Crest City Citizens' Bank. Nothing else.

Steele replaced the wet contents in the wet billfold and put the billfold back in the wet pocket. Then he straightened up and looked along the river, in the direction from which the body – and the gunshot of the night before – had come. It was to the north west, the way he had been headed for the past ten days. He pursed his lips and rasped the back of a hand across the bristles on his jaw. But he remained like that for only a few moments. Then he went to his still unsettled horse and took a blanket and hobble rope from the bedroll. Henry Jaggs began to give off a sickly sweet aroma as he was wrapped in the blanket shroud and then lashed across the front of the gelding's saddle. The animal shook his head as Steele mounted behind the draped burden of the wrapped corpse.

The snort again had a scornful quality.

'I reckon I get your message,' the Virginian said softly as he tugged on the reins to wheel the horse towards the north west. 'But a bank manager is too big a fish to toss back.'

As the sun climbed higher, so its heat mounted. And, beyond the gorge, the terrain was harsher. The going was constantly on an incline, as befitted the route to a place called Crest City. Although the river was always close by to provide the gelding with water, Steele did not ignore the fact that his mount was carrying a double burden. He held the pace to an easy walk and sometimes he dismounted and led the animal by the bridle. But this was as much for his own benefit as that of the horse – to escape for a time the nauseating stench of the corpse fast decomposing in the high heat.

He ate a cold meal at midday and fought against the compulsion to examine his motives. Because of the struggle this entailed, he made the stop a short one. And, during the afternoon, he concentrated on studying the ground close to the banks on each side of the narrowing river: searching for a sign which would betray where the murdered Jaggs had been tossed into the water.

Afternoon was dimming towards evening when he located the spot, on the same, western, side of the river he was travelling, the ground was rocky, with just a scattering of earthy pockets where tufts of grass sprouted. Some of these tufts had been trampled by shod hooves, but there were more telling signs. Two half-smoked cigarettes stained by saliva at their unburnt ends; a cigar butt; a pile of horse droppings; and a stain of splashed blood, dried from its original crimson to an irregular patch of brown.

Steele dismounted again here, and spent a full five minutes surveying the immediate area. The examination told him that there had been at least half a dozen riders involved in the murder of Jaggs, and perhaps as many as ten. They had ridden fast from the north west and, after the killing, had made good time away from the scene – striking out due west towards twin peaks which were now silhouetted cones atop otherwise smooth ridges against the sinking sun.

Back in the saddle, with the high country air cooling, the Virginian demanded a canter from the gelding. And the horse responded eagerly, as if aware that the sooner the ride ended, the sooner he would be rid of the now stiffen-

13

ing corpse slumped across the base of his neck. The river began to inscribe wide curves now, on the line of least resistance across a stretch of country that was almost barren of vegetation. Several dry stream courses ran down to the banks on either side, showing where the Uintas' peaks shed their excess water.

Steele no longer followed the river as it narrowed and shallowed. Instead, he kept to the trail marked by signs showing the way taken by the killers of Henry Jaggs to the place of execution. The sky in the west became bathed in a crimson light as the trailing arc of the sun dipped out of sight. A pale moon put in a tentative appearance on the far side of the sky. The gelding topped a long rise and Steele saw Crest City ahead of him and over to his right.

It stood at the apex of two valleys, one of them with the river flowing through it from its cavernous source and the other an almost featureless vee-shaped rut cut through solid rock. In the valley serviced by year-round water there were a number of farms – clusters of small, neat buildings standing amid fields which were lush with growing crops. A series of trails criss-crossed the valley between paling fences to link the farm-steads: and all of them joined a main trail that climbed the head slope of the two valleys in a series of looping curves to reach Crest City.

In the cool, still air of early evening, columns of smoke rose from farmhouse chimneys, the dark vapour going high before disintegrating in the atmospheric turmoil above the protective sides of the valley. Smoke from the chimneys of Crest City was immediately dispersed. Faint aromas of cooking food reached Steele's nostrils: but never strong enough to mask the stench of putrefying flesh.

Still some three miles from journey's end, the Virginian slowed the pace again. The first half of the final leg was downwards, but the slope was a steep one: initially over weather-smoothed rock and then, lower down, through tangled brush. The men who were to kill Henry Jaggs had adopted a zigzagged course to minimise the steepness of the slope. Steele continued to backtrack their trail.

A shout caused him to halt when he was still several minutes short of the floor of the valley. Night was beginning to take a firm hold on the country now, emerging the less prominent features into their backgrounds. But many lamps had been lit, squaring windows and dropping wedges of yellowness through open doorways. It was in such an open doorway of one of the farmhouses, that Steele saw the silhouetted figure of a man, arm raised to point up at him. As the Virginian watched, two more figures showed against the light – a woman and another man.

One of the men ran from the house doorway and another shout was raised. Other figures appeared against the artificial light spilling from farmhouses. There were more shouts. Steele continued on down the treacherous slope, unable to pick out individual words but detecting the emotions of the agitated farmers and their families. They were anxious, intrigued and excited. They offered no overt threat by either their voices or their actions.

By the time he had reached the floor of the valley the noise had attracted the attention of Crest City's citizens and there was a knot of people standing at the edge of town. And the farmers and their families had formed into another group. Some mounted and most still on foot, they had held back beside the buildings of the farm that was closest to town. They were silent now as the hard brightness of the moon, promising another night frost, showed clearly that the gelding carried more than a single rider. In their silence and reluctance to advance, Steele read fear. Not of any danger he represented: they just did not want to intercept him on the trail and discover too soon what –

or who – was hidden beneath the blanket. They were not close enough to smell the unmistakable clue.

The going was abruptly easier on the valley floor along the hard-packed trail that exploded small puffs of dust from under the gelding's plodding hooves. At the river ford, the horse paused to drink. Then, because of the catty-cornered course up the far side of the valley, the climbing trail was not much of a final obstacle to the travel-wearied gelding.

Crest City and its waiting citizens were lost to sight for most of the upgrade. But, at each sharp turn in the carefully engineered trail, Steele could see the valley people following him from below and matching his appropriately funereal pace to stay the same distance behind him.

Steele rode up the last stretch of the slope and reined the gelding to a halt, blinking his eyes against a sudden dazzle of light.

'Anyone recognise the critter?' a man demanded gruffly.

There was a mumbling of less dominant voices and the resultant sound had a negative tone. Hoofbeats and foot-falls at his back drew Steele to look over his shoulder. The farming people didn't have any lamps to turn up suddenly and hold high. But some of them had handguns and rifles which they levelled at him as they jostled to a halt.

'It sure looks like a dead man, Mr. Mason!' This was from one of the farmers: an old man with a totally bald head and a narrow grey beard that reached down to his belly.

The Virginian showed a wan smile. 'Just tired,' he drawled. 'A bath and a shave and I'll be as bright as morning again.'

The dour and melancholy expressions of the farming families did not alter. As Steele swung to face the front again, the lanterns were lowered and their wicks were

16

turned down. Guns continued to be aimed at him by the men behind the dimmed lights.

'Don't count on it, stranger. Just 'cause you ain't been recognised don't mean you ain't one of the Tyler gang.'

It was the man who had spoken first. He was about fifty with a round face and a belly to match. He had hard, honest-looking dark eyes and sported a bushy moustache that draped low at the corners of his mouth. He was aiming a brass-framed Winchester at Steele and wore a matched pair of ivory-handled Army Colts high on his hips. His star of office was pinned to the breast pocket of his neatly pressed black shirt.

'And iffen you are, you'll be dead and buried dirty and unshaved. Now, you want to climb down out of the saddle, stranger!'

'And no tricks, you hear?'

This threat came from a younger man, who stood immediately beside the sheriff: close enough for the family resemblance to be obvious. He was about twenty-five, with the same round face, a black imitation of the grey moustache and an identical matched pair of Colts. But his handguns were clear of the holsters and levelled at Steele. He had not yet thickened around the middle and his eyes could not generate the same degree of unblinking hardness as those of his father.

Steele pursed his lips and divided an easy glance between both groups of people. 'Like what, kid?' he asked softly. 'Disappear in a puff of smoke?'

'Don't call me a kid!' the youngster snarled as Steele swung out of the saddle.

'Shuddup, Jack!' the lawman growled, and advanced on the gelding as Steele side-stepped away from the horse.

The sheriff rested his Winchester on the ground but all the other drawn guns swung to remain trained upon the Virginian.

'I reckon you ought to clear the ladies off the street before you do that, feller,' Steele advised as the sheriff began to work on the knots holding the blanket in place.

Some of the women gasped and one of them vented a moan – a subdued replica of the howl of the timber wolf. The lawman interrupted what he was doing and looked hard at Steele. Steele met and held the gaze and recognised it as a different brand from before. The lawman had abandoned all preconceived notions and was trying to make an unbiased assessment of the stranger. His expression told nothing of the result, but his tone was less harsh.

'A mess, uh?'

'Shot here,' Steele answered, raising his right hand to point at his temple. He raised the other hand. 'Came out here. It wasn't a ladies' gun. Bullet messed up both his eyes on the way through.'

There were more moans than gasps this time. Some of the sounds came from men.

'That's enough!' the lawman's son warned, thrusting out his Colts with menacing intent.

'Shuddup, Jack!' his father countered. 'The truth shouldn't be hid – from anyone.' He nodded for Steele to continue.

'Happened late last night.' The Virginian lowered his hands and pushed them into the pockets of the sheepskin coat as a gust of wind breathed coldly down Crest City's single street. Only Jack saw danger in the gesture, but a glance around showed he could not expect support from others. 'After he was shot he was put in the river. Current had him for five or six hours. I pulled him out just after sunrise. He started to smell pretty soon after that. It's been a hot day and a long ride.'

The initial shock had passed and the people listened in a brittle silence. It seemed that it wasn't until Steele mentioned the stench of decomposed flesh that the people became aware of it. Nostrils were wrinkled and mouthlines formed into grimaces of revulsion.

'How'd you know when he was shot?' Jack said suddenly. And he had some backing now, as several others matched his suspicious stare at Steele.

The lawman was not one of the tacit accusers, but the Virginian replied to him. 'Heard a shot after I bedded down. When I pulled the body out of the river, I made the connection. He looked dead about that long.'

The sheriff nodded. 'We heard the same shot. Sound carries a mighty long way in these mountains.'

'How'd you know to bring him here to town?' Jack put in, unwilling to accept Steele as easily as his father and the rest of the people.

'Checked his billfold,' Steele told the youngster's father. 'He has some calling cards in it. Named him as Henry Jaggs, the banker in Crest City.'

Gasps hissed from constricted throats again. And a single moan was abruptly curtailed as the woman who vented it slumped into unconsciousness. Two men flanking her caught the body before she thudded to the hard street. The lawman gave Steele a curt nod that combined acknowledgement with acceptance of his story. Then he glanced to left and right at the two groups of watchers. He picked up his Winchester and held it low down, one-handed and not pointing at the Virginian.

'Strange,' he mused. 'All of us here knew it had to be Hank Jaggs under the blanket. But we was all hopeful until you put the name to him.'

'There was life and hope until we knowed he was dead, Mr Mason,' one of the men supporting the unconscious woman said. 'Guess we'd better get Mrs Jaggs to her bed.'

'Do that, Charlie,' Sheriff Mason answered. 'And, Lee, you better take Hank's remains over to your funeral parlour.'

The wind gusted strong enough to raise dust and hurl it in an insubstantial curtain over the gathering as a man moved out of the group on the town side and grasped the gelding's bridle.

'May I use your horse to transport the cadaver?' the mortician asked.

The dust settled and Steele saw that all the guns had been holstered or lowered. Sadness drooped the lines of every face. Only Jack Mason continued to show a trace of suspicion directed at Steele.

'I reckon,' the Virginian told the thin, gaunt-faced Lee. He moved up to the horse and drew the Colt Hartford from the saddle-boot. The inscribed gold stock plate glinted in the moonlight as he canted the rifle to his shoulder. 'Be at the hotel when you're through with him.'

'Mind if I join you?' the lawman asked as both groups began to disperse, the farmers and their families heading back down into the valley and the larger knot untying to move slowly along the street. Except for those directly involved, everyone kept well clear of the dead man and his unconscious widow.

Steele hunched deep inside his coat as he started to amble along the street. 'I don't feel up to entertaining, sheriff,' he said.

'Catchin' up with the Tyler gang won't in no way be entertainment,' the lawman answered as he fell in beside Steele. 'And maybe you can help me do that.'

Jack Mason waited until the two men drew level with him, then moved to take up a position on the other side of Steele.

'I guess you can do some talkin' while you're bathin' and shavin'?' the elder Mason asked.

'Reckon I can,' Steele allowed. 'But it seems to me time your boy was in bed.'

Jack Mason vented a deep growl of anger. 'See here, mister –'

'Shuddup, Jack!' his father cut in. 'This is official law business. Get to the house and take care of supper.'

'But, Pa . . .' the youngster whined.

'Do it!'

Jack angled away from the centre of the street, mumbling to himself as he caressed the butts of his matched Colts.

'You got to make allowances for him,' the sheriff said, a little sadly. 'A few years back I earned myself a reputation as a peace officer down in the south west. Jack figures he's got to try and live up to it.'

The Virginian watched the tall, strongly built youngster go through a lighted doorway under a sign that proclaimed: LAW OFFICE. 'Has his big mouth impressed anyone yet?'

The lawman sighed, the gesture expanding his girth even more. 'He's young. He'll learn.'

Steele nodded. 'But maybe the hard way. And he won't get any older.'

CHAPTER TWO

THE Skyliner wasn't much of a hotel, but then Crest City wasn't much of a town. Just a single street flanked by buildings that were mostly frame business premises with living quarters on the upper storeys or out back. There was the Citizens' Bank which had lost its manager, the law office, the stage depot, a line of stores and a church on one side of the street. Facing these was the telegraph office, the Farmers Association building, the corn exchange, the funeral parlour, livery stable and blacksmith's and the combined saloon, restaurant and hotel. There were only three private houses and these were a few yards north of town, standing behind picket fences at the side of the trail which snaked out from where the street ended.

Crest City had no sidewalks but the Skyliner boasted a covered stoop. The footfalls of Steele and the sheriff rang hollowly on the boarding as the two men stepped up from the street and pushed in through the batswing doors. The saloon and restaurant were both parts of the same room and there was no hotel desk. A bartender with a pock-marked face and an eyepatch checked in Steele and gave him a key with a tag numbered five. The man was not happy that no drinks were called for. He had no other customers using the scarred tables in the big room with the bare wooden walls and smoke-stained ceiling.

'Tonight, I could have saved myself the trouble of lightin' the stoves,' he called sourly as Steele and Mason went up the unrailed stairway which canted along the end wall of the room.

'Boil me some bath water on one of them,' the Virginian answered.

'Be twenty-five cents extra for the trouble,' the bartender countered.

'Trust me for a quarter,' Steele told him. 'I don't want any trouble.'

All the doors on the upper floor were open, showing that Steele was the Skyliner's sole guest. Room five was at the front of the building, with a window looking out over the bottle-littered stoop roof into the street. It was as spartanly decorated and underfurnished as the saloon and restaurant. Just a double bed, a bureau with a cracked mirror and a padded rocking chair. There was no carpet to cover the bare boards. But they were clean, and so were the sheets on the bed.

Sheriff Mason sank wearily into the chair, rested his Winchester across the split arms and began to rock himself. After Steele had lit the ceiling-hung lamp and taken off his top coat and hat, the lawman eyed him appraisingly.

'You look like you talk, stranger.'

'How's that?'

Mason took out a cheroot and held it up for permission to smoke it. Steele nodded as he tested the bed. 'Like a man who's seen better days and stayed at better places than this.'

'And worse days and worse places than this,' Steele allowed. 'But a man has to take the rough with the smooth.'

There were more sounds of footfalls on the hotel's stoop as men came in off the street.

'Life in this town was pretty smooth up until yesterday afternoon,' Mason said on a cloud of aromatic blue smoke. 'Never plush and easy, but with no bad trouble.'

'Hit the bank and took Jaggs as hostage to keep you from following?' Steele suggested.

'Almost right,' the sheriff replied. 'But I wasn't here in town. Jack and me were up in the high peaks. Blue Pool Lake. Fishing. Didn't know nothin' about the bank raid until Lee McNally rode up and told us what happened.'

'You came back, but didn't take out a posse?'

The old harshness re-entered Mason's dark eyes. But this time the expression was of resentment to criticism. Footfalls and heavy breathing sounded out in the hallway and the bartender came into the room, hauling a hip tub.

'Wife'll bring up the water when it's hot.'

'Only kind of hot water I want to get in,' Steele told Mason after the man with the eyepatch had left the room. 'Just stating a fact.'

The sheriff accepted this with a nod. 'It was the Tyler gang. Headed by a mad dog sonofabitch named Olney Tyler. I could cover every wall in every room of this hotel with the wanted bills I got on that bunch. I figured sure as night follows day they wouldn't turn old Hank Jaggs loose when they was clear. But the folks in Crest City and down in the valley – they outvoted me. And it almost came to a vote, to toss me outta the office of peace officer.'

He drew hard against his cheroot, then cupped a hand to knock ash into a palm. The bartender's wife was more discreet than her husband. Neither man was aware of her approach until she came into the room, a two-gallon pail of steaming water in each hand. Steele's heritage as a Virginian gentleman was betrayed again when he stood on seeing the woman. She was ten years junior to her husband, with a statuesque body but a face that was too careworn to be attractive. She smiled as if unfamiliar with the expression when Steele took the water from her to empty it into the tub. She smelled as clean as Steele wanted to be. At the doorway on her exit, she halted.

'Somethin', mister.'

'What's that?'

'I didn't hear no one say thanks to you for fetchin' in Hank's body. The whole town is much obliged to you for that. I guess everyone'll tell you the same when the shock's over.'

'I can't say it was a pleasure, ma'am,' Steele replied.

'I'll get more water,' the woman said quickly, and hurried out, as silently as she had come.

'That's been puzzlin' me, stranger.'

'What has, sheriff?'

'Why you brought him in.'

Steele took off his jacket and vest. He showed a mirthless smile. 'It'd be easy to say it seemed like a good idea at first. But it sure stank later.'

'Don't make jokes about Hank Jaggs being killed,' Mason said evenly. 'He was a much loved man around here. Valley's lookin' mighty prosperous now, but there's been some bad years. And when the weather flattens the crops or dries them so they won't grow, town businesses suffer as much as the homesteaders. Hank's bank holds papers on most every square inch of property and buildin' lumber around here. And he never foreclosed nor charged high interest nor even hurried a man who couldn't pay on time.'

Mason's cheroot wasn't tasting good any more. As the overworked woman came back into the room with enough water to fill the tub, the sheriff went to the window, opened it and tossed out the cheroot and handful of ash. A cold draught lanced into the room and swirled the steam towards the door.

'Grateful to you, ma'am,' Steele told the woman.

'Least I can do,' she answered, and closed the door behind her on the way out.

25

At a sign from Steele, Mason jerked the drapes across the window and then the Virginian completed removing his clothes. The lawman returned to the chair and resumed rocking himself. Naked, Steele lowered himself into the steaming water, grimacing in first reaction to the heat, then smiling with relish. The woman had left a neatly folded towel and a tablet of soap on the bed. As Steele reached for the soap, the lawman did not fail to notice that the Colt Hartford was also on the bed, within easy reaching distance.

'You're not telling me all this to explain her gratitude, sheriff,' the Virginian said as he started to soap his hands, arms and torso.

Mason sighed, tried to hold Steele's enquiring gaze, but failed. He looked down at his big hands fisted around the stock and barrel of the Winchester. 'Jack ain't the only one proud of my reputation, mister. I got my pride, too. And it got some bad dents in it when I had to hold still on account of what folks told me.' He sighed again, and this time met Steele's dark-eyed gaze for a longer period. 'And the truth of it is, I wouldn't want a man like you to think I'm yellow.'

Steele rinsed off the suds and rose to soap the lower half of his body. 'A man who's seen better days and stayed in better places?'

Mason looked as if he was ready to blow up in anger in response to Steele's even-toned answer. But he stared down at his fisted hands and brought himself under control. He shook his head savagely. 'Hell, I ain't much with words, mister. Didn't used to matter in the old days, when it was deeds that were important and I did them. But I'm stale now. Only law trouble I've ever had to handle in Crest City is when Uziel Wadsworth used to get drunk on Saturday nights and disturbed the peace with his singin'. And Uziel's been dead this five years gone.'

26

'You can talk fine, sheriff,' Steele said as he sat down in the tub again. 'But you make circles around your point.'

Mason nodded his agreement, his fleshy face colouring with embarassment. 'Guess that sure is right.'

'Tell you what,' Steele offered. 'You go get me a razor. And, while you're doing it, collect your thoughts. Then, maybe when you get back here, you'll be able to get right to the point and ask me what you . . . .'

'Okay,' Mason said quickly, springing to his feet.

As Steele stepped from the bath tub, the lawman hurried to the door, as if the Virginian was a brazen woman whose nakedness embarrassed the big man. Steele towelled himself dry and dressed in the sweat-stiffened and dusty clothing. Then he sat on the edge of the bed and counted up the value of his slender bankroll. It didn't take long. Just fifteen one dollar bills: which was not enough to buy even a pair of boots of the kind he favoured.

Mason took ten minutes to run the errand and when he returned he had both a razor and some regular shaving soap. 'It's my stuff,' he said as the Virginian began to work on the long bristles. 'Wouldn't want folks to know I was runnin' around on the say-so of a stranger –'

'You made the point about your pride, feller,' the Virginian put in, leaning over the bathtub to ensure the bristle-speckled soap came off the razor into the dirty water.

Mason had resumed his gun-toting posture in the rocking chair. 'Hell!' he exclaimed. 'Olney Tyler and his nine men rode into Crest City at three o'clock yesterday afternoon. Moved into the bank and drew guns on Hank Jaggs and his wife and two customers. Took better than ten thousand dollars outta the safe and left. Took Hank with them and said they'd hold him for twenty-fours hours then turn him loose. As a hostage to stop anyone fixin' to trail them.'

He lit another cheroot and its lighted end glowed

27

brightly, as if manifesting the fact that the lawman was warming to his subject now he had launched into it directly. 'When Lee McNally came up to Blue Pool Lake to tell me what had happened, I didn't set no store by what the Tyler gang promised. Like I told you, mister, I got a whole stack of wanted bills on that bunch. And if one of them told me the moon wasn't made of blue cheese, I'd want to take a bite at it first before I'd believe him.'

Steele completed shaving and Mason felt free to make use of the bath tub. As he continued to talk, the ash from his cheroot began to litter the scummy surface of the water.

'So I wanted to take off after the gang right away. But wasn't anyone but Jack ready to ride with me. And the rest of the folks around here. . . .' He grimaced. 'Well, first they said they'd vote me outta office. Then there was a threat they wouldn't let me ride out. It wasn't said like that, you understand. But it was there.'

'Implied,' Steele said softly.

'What?'

'I'm better with words than you are,' the Virginian supplied. 'What about the shot you heard last night?'

A shrug of the broad shoulders. 'Wasn't anyone ready to be certain it was aimed at Hank Jaggs. They said to wait the full twenty-four hours. Said it could have been anyone shootin' at anythin'.'

'And at three o'clock this afternoon?'

Mason coloured with embarrassment again and he moved his hands restlessly on the Winchester. 'I guess I can be as stubborn as anybody else around here, mister. They was all for me ridin' out then. But I told them to go to hell. If they had so much faith in the Tyler gang keepin' its word, then Hank Jaggs oughta come back to Crest City under his own steam.'

There was a long pause and Mason looked enquiringly

at the washed but shabby Virginian. Steele gave him a slight nod and an even slighter smile.

'You're talking as well as a Washington politician now, sheriff. Only trouble is, it's getting to be like a Capitol Hill filibuster. And that's for wasting time.'

'Sonofabitch!' Mason hissed, dividing the anger equally between himself and Steele. 'Okay! The townspeople and the farmers were wrong. Then I was wrong. Between us, we lost us a lot of time. And we lost Hank Jaggs. Ain't no way to get back either. All we can do is get the Tyler gang.'

'With my help?' Steele suggested.

Mason almost smiled. His lips parted to show the smoke-stained teeth beneath the bushy moustache. But the dark eyes stopped short on the brink of betraying relief. 'You offerin', mister? I ain't used to askin' for no favours.'

'I'm selling,' the Virginian corrected.

Mason's parted lips formed into the line of a scowl now and he stood up abruptly. 'That don't surprise me none. I knew you was aimin' to collect somethin' for your trouble. A man like you don't haul a stinkin' corpse through the heat of the sun on account of the feelin's of the next of kin.' He shrugged. 'Don't know what your angle was, but if I deputise you, the pay is two dollars daily, and all found.'

Steele had put on his hat and coat while Mason was speaking. Now, in the lengthening pause that followed the outlining of the lawman's terms, the Virginian pulled on the skin-tight black gloves and canted the Colt Hartford to his shoulder. He started towards the door.

'You startin' right now?' Mason called.

'Going to pay my respects to the dead man's next of kin,' Steele answered. He pulled open the door. 'And see if she's prepared to top your offer, sheriff.'

The lines of Mason's scowl deepened. 'You're gonna put the screws on a new widow?' he growled.

29

'Two dollars a day and all found won't be hard to top.'

The sheriff followed him out into the hallway. 'She hasn't got a cent, mister. The Tyler gang took it all.'

Steele nodded as they walked side by side towards the head of the stairs. 'So Mrs Jaggs ought to be willing to pay ten cents on every dollar I get back from the Tyler bunch, I reckon.'

Mason recognised there was no point to further anger and he nodded in agreement with a thought that had just struck him. 'A man like you, it's the way it has to be. Nothin' for nothin'. Anythin' for as much as you can get!' He dropped the stub of his cheroot on a stairway tread and crushed it out with his heel as he started downwards. 'Guess it would be too much to expect you to have any principles.'

The bartender with an eyepatch, his life-harrowed wife and the saloon's dozen or so customers who had now come in watched the Virginian and the sheriff bleakly as the two men reached the foot of the stairway. The saloon, with its two pot-bellied stoves glowing crimson, was luxuriously warm after the chill of the unheated upstairs room.

'Principles are the interest on the principal, feller,' Steele said as he crossed towards the batswing doors while Mason angled towards the bar.

The philosophy was lost upon the eavesdroppers, who continued to treat the Virginian to a barrage of flat stares.

'You leavin' us, mister?' the bartender's wife called.

'Don't bother him now, Flora,' Mason growled, pointing to a whiskey bottle. 'Only question that concerns that critter is one of money.'

'That makes sense,' the woman replied dully.

Steele touched the brim of his hat and smiled at her over his shoulder. 'Hoping to do better than that, ma'am. Reckon to make dollars.'

CHAPTER THREE

Hank Jaggs was lowered to his final resting place at an hour past sunrise the next morning. Only the preacher and the widow of the dead man concentrated their full attention upon the elongated pine box lying at the bottom of the open grave. The others among the large group of sombrely garbed and gaunt-faced mourners were unable to resist the compulsion to glance out of the small churchyard towards the front of the Skyliner Hotel.

For most of the interment ceremony, there was nothing to see before the hotel except a line of nine horses hitched to the rail. But then, as the preacher began to intone the final prayer for Jagg's soul and the church bell started to toll the death knell, the owners of the horses pushed out through the batswings.

Sheriff Mason and his son were in the forefront of the posse. Behind them came a motley band of Crest City citizens and valley farmers. Adam Steele emerged from the saloon last of all and at first glance there was just a single factor which set him apart from the rest – there was no lawman's star pinned to his chest.

All the mourners knew the reason for this as the funeral service continued and the posse mounted, slid rifles into saddle-boots and unhitched the reins of their horses from the rail. Hank's widow had agreed to the Virginian's terms of a ten per cent reward on whatever money he could recover from the Tyler gang. Word of this had been circulated last night while Steele was going to sleep in a

31

regular bed for the first time in many days. But it had been late after a long, tension-filled day and there had been little talk beyond this.

This morning, though, as the mourners gathered in the tiny churchyard, there had been a great deal of speculation about the southern-talking stranger: particularly in relation to why Crest City's sheriff wanted him along on the hunt for vengeance.

For that was what it was. Everyone who watched the posse canter out of town and start down the zigzagging trail to the valley floor knew this. Likewise the badge-carrying men in the hunting party. The money which the Tyler gang had taken from the bank safe was a bad second to the desire to avenge Hank Jaggs's death.

On the far side of the valley, the men had to dismount for the climb up the steep slope. The slow tolling of the death knell from the church tower was like a signal from which the nine-man posse measured their laboured pace.

'Them thieving bastards had to hoof it this way,' Charlie Risby said. 'And all we could do was stand and watch 'em!'

Across the broad apex formed by the barren valley and the fertile one, watching eyes followed the progress of the second group of men to scale the dangerous gradient. The bell had ceased to toll its mournful message of death and burial and the undivided attention of every mourner was focused upon the posse.

At the top, from where Steele had gained his first sight of Crest City and the farming land spread out beneath, the men remounted. Some waved across the wide depression and received answering gestures.

'Your party, Steele,' Mason invited.

'I don't see why it has to be, Pa,' his son growled.

'Me neither, Mr Mason,' Dexter Spelling added.

Spelling, the farmer with the long grey beard, and Charlie

32

Risby, the town's muscular blacksmith, were in the same upper middle-age group as the sheriff. The rest of the men fell between the ages of Jack Mason and Steele. Royd Carpenter and Lawton Morgan were both farmers' sons. Gil Trapp was the telegraph operator and Quinn Lamont the stage depot manager. All of them either nodded their agreement or made their views just as clear by abstaining from any kind of gesture.

'Because he knows where Hank was shot and the Tyler bunch lit off from the southbound route they was takin'!' Mason snarled. 'Steele can get us there fast without no need to waste time trackin'!'

He glowered around at his sworn deputies and each of them tacitly expressed that there was no argument against this. Then his features stayed set in hard lines as he stared at Steele.

'Okay, let's move. There's been time lost sleepin' now.'

'Everybody has to sleep, feller,' the Virginian replied evenly as he heeled the gelding forward. 'Even men who are ten grand rich.'

'Which proves that money ain't everythin',' Mason countered with a note of triumph as he moved in close behind Steele.

'There's all kinds of sleep,' the Virginian argued and the lawman was not prepared to take the discussion any further.

As it happened, tracking the Tyler gang's cold trail to the point at the river bank where Jaggs was murdered would have been slow and difficult. The wind and frost of the previous night had destroyed much of the signs and it would have been necessary to follow the meandering course of the widening and deepening river – trusting to luck that the posse did not overshoot the all important turning point.

But, with Steele to show the way, the nine men were able

to make good time on a virtually straight course. And the pace began to have its effects on some of the men before they were halfway to their first objective. The Virginian was the only member of the posse recently familiar with the rigours of hard riding across rugged terrain beneath the cruel heat of the sun. By the nature of their jobs, the blacksmith Risby and the three farmers – Spelling, Carpenter and Morgan – were tougher than the rest. Thus, it was the younger men and the underworked sheriff who were the first to show signs of distress. Like the telegraph man, Trapp, and Lamont who ran the stage depot, Jack Mason also earned his keep with an easy, inside job – he worked in the Crest City Hardware Store.

First they got saddle sore. Then they began to sweat too much from wide open pores in highly coloured skin. Finally, as they sucked too often and too much from their canteens, their high colour faded to paleness. The lawman handled his problems best, calling upon the experiences of his heyday and by using sheer will power.

At a watering stop for the horses and for the men to refill their canteens, the elder Mason moved across to where the Virginian had just finished relieving himself.

'You don't have to prove nothin' to me, mister!' he rasped through teeth clenched around an unlit cheroot. 'I wanted you along 'cause I knowed you were the right kinda man for a job like this. But in provin' it to these guys you could run them into the ground before we're closer than twenty miles to the Tyler bunch.'

He made to light the cheroot, but the low-voiced warning had taken a lot of effort and he was wheezing rather than breathing. He looked his age and more as he sagged against a rock, seemingly pushed against the support by the power emanating from the Virginian's expressionless eyes.

'That's your problem, feller,' Steele said softly, absently rubbing the back of a gloved hand over his smooth-shaved jaw. 'It's your posse and I'm not a part of it. You fellers just happen to be riding the same way I am.'

'And you damn well know why!' Mason yelled after sucking in a deep breath.

His raised voice silenced several conversations among the other men. Every pair of eyes swung to look towards the lawman and the Virginian. For stretched seconds, Mason's anger stayed high, with plenty to spare from Steele to spill towards the others.

Jack Mason dropped both hands to drape the butts of his holstered Colts. He swung sideways-on towards Steele and glared menacingly at the Virginian. 'This pint-size dude givin' you trouble, Pa?' he snapped.

'He doesn't deserve any more, kid,' Steele replied evenly. 'Not after his wife gave him you.'

'Why you. . . .'

The younger Mason was fast and smooth on the draw. The guns came free of the holsters simultaneously and the hammers were cocked at precisely the right moment. But he was exhausted from the ride and he was angry. His hands shook. The twin barrels wavered from side to side and jiggled up and down.

'Shuddup, Jack!' his father barked. 'And put them guns away!'

The younger man shook his head and his lower lip trembled as much as his hands. 'No, Pa. You taught me to draw like this. There had to come a time when it would be in earnest.'

The sheriff took two steps which put his bulky form between the guns and Steele. 'I also taught you when not to draw, son,' he said, his breathing and voice controlled now. 'There's lots of times when not to. One is against an unarmed man.'

Jack Mason blinked and leaned to the side, looking

around his father. Steele had been riding minus both his sheepskin coat and his suit jacket. His narrow waistline was blatantly minus a gunbelt. The youngster looked towards the gelding and blinked gain – this time as sunlight danced on the gold stock plate of the booted rifle. Then he pouted as he thrust the Colts back in their holsters.

'He's gettin' to me, Pa. First he smart mouths me, then he starts in on you.'

The lawman took a long time to fight back the anger which threatened to rise within him again. The voice of the tall and skinny Quinn Lamont ended the pause.

'I figured we came out here to fight the Tyler gang. Not squabble amongst ourselves.'

Mason announced his readiness to speak with a determined nod of his head. 'That's just what we come out here for!' he agreed, raking a level stare around every member of the posse except Steele, who was still standing nonchalantly behind him. 'But without a man like Steele, we don't have a chance against that bunch. And Steele's the only one of his kind we got.'

'What the hell kind is he, Pa?' Jack Mason growled.

'The killin' kind, I'd say,' the boy's father replied at once. 'The same kind as Olney Tyler and them that rides with him.'

The sheriff stepped away from Steele now, like a ring master who has introduced the star attraction in a show. The small audience of deputies reacted by looking hard at the Virginian, as if seeing him for the first time. Steele submitted to the examination for no more than two seconds. Then he stepped away from the rock with its stain of dried urine and angled among the men to where the horses were waiting after drinking their fill.

'You men have led sheltered lives,' the sheriff went on. 'Maybe the first mean bastards you ever saw was when the

Tyler bunch hit Crest City. And then you was all too damn scared to take a real good look at them. Well, I seen a thousand men like the Tyler bunch when I was – '

'Pa!' his son cut in, at once pleading and angry.

Steele swung up into his saddle, aware that most of the men had switched their attention away from him to survey the lawman. Now he looked at the elder Mason and saw what had caused the youngster's concern. The sheriff had surrendered to the effects of the long, hard ride. The soft, overweight man was sitting on the rock, resting his cupped hands on his fleshy thighs. Exhaustion added even more years to his age. The only part of him which didn't sag was his head. This was held high, to display his face for all to see. Tears coursed over the curves of his cheeks along with the sweat beads, but they had not erupted from any physical pain.

'. . . like the Tyler bunch and Steele,' he continued, as if he had not heard the urgent shout from his son.

'You was a killer, Mr Mason?' the blond-haired, fresh-faced Gil Trap gasped incredulously.

'Use the sense you was born with, son,' Dexter Spelling responded tightly, his long beard swinging from side to side as he shook his head. 'What the sheriff is tryin' to say is – '

'And I'll say it, Goddamn it!' the lawman barked, pushing himself to his feet. He brushed a big hand across his face and wiped off the tears. The familiar hardness was back in his eyes. 'Some things I still don't need help with.' He glowered around him, tacitly commanding that there be no further interruptions. Then he nodded his satisfaction of, and into, the silence.

'I killed men, sure. But in the name of the law when they wouldn't get caught no other way. I hunted them and I brung them in – dead or alive. I had to be as tough and as hard and as mean as them or I wouldn't be here today. But that was all a long time ago a long ways from here. And since then I got fat and weak and tired and even lazy, maybe.'

Jack seemed set to cut across his father's speech again, but the sheriff sensed the boy's intention and drove him back into tight-lipped silence with a powerful stare.

'If I wasn't all them things, I wouldn't have held still in Crest City two days ago. But I did hold still, Goddamn it. And the longer I held still, the more I knew I was all them things. Then Steele rode in with Hank's body and I saw in him the way I was.' He sagged back against the rock, 'And the way I can never be again.'

Jack curtailed the lengthening silence. 'That's crazy, Pa!' he yelled. 'You're older, is all. But there ain't no rush. The pint-size dude is right there. The way the Tyler bunch operate, we'll catch up with 'em – sooner or later. And when we do, you'll handle it. With seven guys ready and willing to give you any help you need.'

Everyone was well rested now and a lot of the weariness of the ride had been dissipated. The farmers and the inside workers nodded enthusiastically.

'Ready and willing anytime to make 'em pay for what they did to Hank, Mr Mason!' the rangy Quinn Lamont agreed.

The sheriff eyed the bored-looking Virginian who had sat silently astride his horse during the exchange. 'How do you figure that, feller?' he asked.

Steele pursed his lips. 'I reckon they're ready and willing, all right,' he allowed. 'But I have my doubts about whether they're able.'

The lawman started a slow nod of agreement and some of the others made sounds of dissent. But a growl of frustrated anger exploded from Jack Mason. All eyes swung towards him as he ripped off his hat. Then he went down into a crouch, whipped erect and scaled the hat high into the air. Steele and the sheriff expressed sourness in equal degree while the others watched in amazement.

Jack Mason exhibited his fast double draw again: and this time the matched Colts exploded. Eight bullets were spun towards the flying hat as steady fingers squeezed the triggers alternately. Three hit the target while it was still ascending. The other five altered the course of the falling hat. It was pushed out over the river and splashed down into the water ten feet from the bank.

'Every one of 'em through the brim!' Jack boasted, his voice pitched high with excited pride. 'Who ain't able?'

He glared at Steele.

The Virginian pursed his lips. 'You ever tried it when there was a head in the hat, kid?' he asked.

Jack holstered his guns and extended his arms, palms uppermost and fingers splayed. "What the hell have I got to do?' he demanded.

'Go get your hat back,' his father replied sadly.

'And reload the fancy guns,' Steele added. He clucked to the gelding and dug in his heels gently to urge the animal forward.

'You sure do a lot of pushin' for a guy in no rush, Steele,' Mason accused as his son stepped off the bank and plunged immediately into deep water.

'I said there was no rush for you fellers,' Steele corrected. 'But time is money for me. I lose ten cents on every dollar the Tyler bunch spends.'

'Mount up, you guys!' Mason ordered as Steele faced front to steer his horse along a grassy pathway through a scattering of sun-bleached rocks. 'Like it or not, we're with him.'

Jack Mason could swim as well as he shot. Fully clothed, he made good time to his hat and back to the river bank. He climbed out, dripping water, and jammed the hat back on his head. Sunlight shafted through the eight bullet holes to dapple his neck and shoulders with irregular spots of yellow.

'It sure oughta have proved somethin',' he yelled as he leapt into his saddle and galloped his mare to catch up with the departing group.

'It proved you got a hatful of holes, son,' his father growled.

'And that he's more than just wet behind the ears,' the Virginian muttered, the clop of trotting hooves masking his words from the others.

CHAPTER FOUR

THE posse was two and a half days out of Crest City when the sheriff, his deputies and the loner in the crowd caught up with the Tyler bunch. From the Hank Jaggs murder scene, where the bank robbers swung away from the river to head west, progress had been slow. For it was necessary to start really tracking the fugitives, across barren mountain terrain that favoured the pursued above their pursuers. Most of the way to the distant twin peaks and across the broad plateau beyond, the country was composed of solid rock which reared and dipped in a petrified maelstrom which seemed purposely formed to hide all sign of the passage of horses and riders.

Thus, it was no longer the pace of the pursuit that wearied the posse. Nor was it the concentrated effort of seeking the infrequent sign – for, by common consent after he had proved his ability, the tracking chore was left entirely to the Virginian. Rather, it was the physical effects of the blazing heat of day and the bitter cold of night, in exhausting combination with the mental repercussions of boredom and frustration.

But, in this respect, the sheriff showed his worth above the deputies. For, although the extremes of weather hit him as hard as the others, the lessons of past experience enabled him to stay mentally alert at all times.

'Could be up there,' Steele said as he led the posse through the fading light of evening towards a natural arch of rock at the foot of a long, open, shallow slope.

41

'Like they could have been at a dozen other places that gave you the shakes, dude?' Jack Mason taunted, his sun-reddened face contorting into the lines of a hateful sneer.

'Shuddup, boy!' his father growled, following the direction of Steele's appraising gaze.

'But, Mr Mason!' Royd Carpenter said wearily. 'That pile of horseshit we saw a mile back is at least twelve hours outta the nag.'

Both the Virginian and the lawman ignored the complaint as they rode under the arch of rock and raked their dark eyes up the slope. At the crest there was a long run of sheer cliff face, jagged at the top and split in just one place to form the mouth of what looked like a canyon. As they started up the rise, Steele glanced back over his shoulder. Spread out behind them, to an horizon foreshortened by falling darkness, was the vast flatness of the western half of the plateau.

'Someone up on the cliff would have had us in sight near all day,' Mason muttered, voicing the thought which he knew was in Steele's mind.

'Hell, Pa!' Jack Mason exclaimed, and spat. 'Them guys are better than four days clear of Crest City. And they're rich. They ain't gonna expect us to chase them. And when they stop, it'll be someplace they can use the money they stole.'

'Steele ain't sayin' they're up there!' the sheriff countered. 'Just that they could be. So you guys better stay watchful and ready.'

It was full night when the riders reached the top of the rise. The moon was up and just a sliver away from perfect roundness. But it was low and only a narrow edge of its light reached into the mouth of the canyon. The clop of the horses' hooves resounded off the facing walls of the cliff.

But, deeper into the towering rocks, the canyon broadened and its floor became softer, rock and hard-packed dirt giving way to springy turf. More moonlight spilled over the northern rim and the riders heard the melodic sound of running water. The horses smelled the answer to their thirst and attempted to ignore the restraint of tight-held reins. The men had been rationed as frugally as their mounts and many of them licked their lips in keen anticipation as they listened to the tantalising splashing sound.

'Over there!' Spelling said, abruptly and loudly, pointing ahead and to the right.

Nobody needed the excited direction. The light of the moon picked out clearly the spring that spouted from twenty feet up the canyon wall, the white water tumbling down into a pool and then forming a narrow stream across the floor to disappear into a cave on the far side.

'Man, that's gonna taste even better than One-Eyed Sam's beer at the end of Midsummer's Day!' Lawton Morgan exclaimed, and slammed in his heels.

'Hold it!' Steele yelled.

'Morgan, do like – ' Mason started.

But he gave up when the rest of his deputies vented their excitement and drove their mounts fast towards the pool. The canyon was suddenly filled with hectic sound as the thirsty snorts of the animals were added to the cacophony.

'Well, maybe we cried wolf too many times, mister!' Mason said to Steele, having to shout even though just four feet separated their stationary horses.

A gunshot blasted a violent full point to the lawman's comment. The young Morgan was sent into a cartwheel as he tried to leap from his horse to the side of the splashing pool. Scattering pellets from a shotgun tore into the flesh of his head, shoulders and chest as crimson spray exploded from him to stain the water.

'Who's crying now?' Steele yelled as he kicked free of his stirrups, snatched the rifle from its boot and dived from the horse.

As if in direct response to the rasping query, Morgan vented a death scream as he plunged into the pool.

The sheriff was slower, but the next three shots which blasted all other sounds into apparent silence were not aimed at him. Unlike the shotgun blast, they did not come from the top of a grassy knoll which rose thirty feet beyond the pool. They were exploded by rifles and the muzzle flashes stabbed orange from within the dark mouth of the cave. One of the shots smashed into the bulging eye of Morgan's rearing horse. The animal crashed down on to all fours again and then started to topple. But the big Charlie Risby and the blond Gil Trapp beat the horse to the ground. Both men took the bullets in their chests as they whipped around in their saddles, eyes seeking out the attackers as hands reached for rifles.

'The bastards!' Jack Mason screamed, drawing his Colts and getting off two shots before he threw himself from his horse.

The shots were impulsive and went wild. But they acted as a spur to Spelling, Carpenter and Lamont. The trio fell, rather than jumped from their horses. Another burst of gunfire, from the knoll, the cave mouth and the canyon rim above the spring, brought down Spelling's gelding. But the animal managed a half-dozen panicked paces before he started to roll, dragging his rider by a foot trapped in the stirrup. Man and beast were in the shallow stream with water clouded by Morgan's blood. Spelling shrieked with the agony of crushed ribs as the dead weight of the animal smashed down onto him.

'The cave!' Steele yelled to Mason as he and the lawman dived into a hollow after a sprint from where they left their horses.

Mason grunted an acknowledgement and began to pump and fire the brass-framed Winchester at the specified target. The Virginian rolled over onto his back and the Colt Hartford spat lead up towards the canyon rim.

For long moments, the hail of bullets interrupted further attacking shots from above and to the north.

'Get back here!' Mason yelled, then cursed as his own and Steele's horse bolted across his line of fire.

Shots roared from inside the cave and both horses were stopped dead in their gallop and went into snorting, kicking rolls.

Jack Mason, Quinn Lamont and Royd Carpenter rose in unison, blasted towards the knoll, turned and ran towards the hollow. The shotgun exploded its roaring voice again and Carpenter began to leave a trail of blood in his wake as he ran and screamed.

Steele dropped his empty rifle and snatched one of the Colts from the lawman's holster. As he rolled back, he caught a glimpse of a face at the top of the knoll. A gaunt, skull-like face with eyes so deep set that the sockets appeared to be empty. With long, prominent teeth that shone in a maniacal grin of triumph. The gun muzzle below the face expelled a stab of orange and Quinn Lamont pitched forward out of his run. The bullet which had taken him in the back of the neck had enough velocity to burrow through his lower head and burst clear through his open, screaming mouth. As he fell, following the arc of his spilled blood, Mason's Winchester rattled empty. In the time it took the lawman to draw and fire the first shot from his remaining Colt, a further fusillade of gunfire rained out of the cave.

Royd Carpenter took four bullets in his head and torso and was flung to the side by the impact. His dead body crashed into the running Jack Mason and the lawman's son vented a high-pitched scream of terror as he was

45

splashed with warm blood and felt himself knocked off his feet.

'Jack!' the sheriff shrieked.

'Stay down!' Steele warned.

But his words went unheeded. Mason flung aside his revolver and whipped upright to haul himself out of the hollow.

'I'm okay, Pa!' Jack yelled, struggling to get out from under the dead weight of Carpenter.

But nobody heard the words. Hoofbeats were again loud in the canyon. Different animals from a different direction. And the sharp crack of gunfire counterpointed the dull thud of metal against turf.

Four mounted men galloped from the mouth of the cave. Three riderless horses were forced to match the headlong pace, led by ropes lashed around the saddlehorns of three of those that were mounted. All four galloping men fired. Other shots exploded from the knoll. Still more ambushers poured down lead from the high rim of the canyon.

Sheriff Mason was a fast moving target, but he was a big one. One bullet creased his forehead and curtained blood down over his eyes. Two more drilled into his left thigh and he was stopped, turned and pushed into a fall. Finally, three drove deep into his lower belly.

Neither Steele nor the lawman's son saw this, for both pressed themselves flat against the ground to get under the spray of flying lead. Then, as the fire abruptly ended, they raised only their heads and gun-hands. Their targets were the mounted men, and the three still on foot who broke from the cover of the knoll and raced towards the led animals.

But the range was better than sixty feet and they had only the Army Colts. An ambusher's horse snickered as it was creased across the hindquarters by a lucky shot. Then the running men were clear of the ground and slamming into their saddles as the ropes were unhitched. Like a

46

distant echo, more hoofbeats sounded along the canyon rim.

'Nobody tangles with the Tyler boys without wishin' they hadn't!'

The taunt was shouted down into the canyon, and was followed by a burst of high-pitched, almost feminine laughter.

Two shots rang out, but neither of the bullets were aimed at human targets. A pair of geldings which had been ridden by Lamont and Jack Mason had bolted to apparant safety. But their quivering silhouettes were spotted in a patch of deep moon shadow and they died from well-placed rifle shots exploded at the full gallop.

'Pa!' the younger Mason shrieked, aware for the first time his father had been hit.

He lifted Carpenter's blood-drenched body off his legs and hurled it aside. Then he stumbled in a half-crouch to where the lawman lay, almost motionless except for an exhausted rise and fall of his chest.

'Pa, you're gonna be all right!' the youngster said with grim determination as he raised his father's head and worked a leg under it. 'Ain't he gonna be all right, mister?'

Steele ignored the unanswerable query, raking his eyes in every direction as he ejected the spent shells from the Colt Hartford's chambers and fed in fresh ones. Then he stood, and continued to survey his surroundings as he eased out of the hollow. The sounds of the ambushers' departure had now completely faded. But there was no guarantee that a man or two had not been left to look after careless survivors.

'Look at him, will you?' the youngster demanded. 'Tell me what I can do for him?'

Steele let out a long pent-up breath. There was still no physical guarantee that the killing was over. But he had a feel about the presence or absence of potential danger. A kind of sixth sense which he had discovered during the bloody War Between the States and developed in the violent peace which followed. It was not always accurate – had given him false responses at all the other possible ambush points until this canyon. But he elected to trust it now. To an extent.

'What can I do to help him?' Jack Mason pleaded again, turning his tear-stained face up to look at the Virginian.

Steele relaxed his surveillance for a moment to glance down at the father and son. He discounted the face and leg wounds, but the big patch of blood on the lawman's belly and the sound and cadence of the injured man's breathing drew a negative gesture from him.

'Pray, is all,' he said softly, and moved away to check on the other members of the posse.

'You been around, Steele!' Mason yelled after him. 'You're supposed to be so smart! There's gotta be somethin' better than that we can do!'

The staring, pain and terror-filled eyes of Lamont and Carpenter made it blatantly obvious that the stage depot manager and the farmer were dead. Risby lay face down, but was as inert as the ground upon which he was sprawled. Morgan had been under the surface of the pool for far too long still to be alive. Steele dragged out the sodden bulk of the farmer so that the water would become unfouled. Gil Trapp called softly for his mother, then died with blood bubbling from his mouth as Steele was about to squat beside him. The bearded Spelling had been drowned, his face forced into the stream by the weight of his dead horse.

'Answer me, dude!' Jack Mason screamed. Carpenter's discarded rifle lay on the ground nearby and the youngster snatched it up and aimed it at Steele.

The Virginian was in the process of checking on the horses now. The eight he could see were all on their sides and dead. He was looking down on his own blood-smeared gelding when the lawman's son yelled the demand. He turned his head in time to see the sheriff raise a weary hand, hook it over the barrel and drag the rifle down from the aim. Jack immediately released the weapon and took his father's face in his hands.

'Ain't nothin' nobody can do for me on this earth no more, son,' the elder Mason rasped.

Because of the splashing of the falling water into the pool, Steele did not hear the words. But, with the threat of the aimed rifle removed, he ignored the father and son and peered up and down the canyon, half moonlit and half in shadow. He couldn't see the missing horse, but he decided the animal had bolted into a backtrack away from the sound of gunfire, stench of burnt powder and scent of fresh-spilled blood.

Jack Mason was talking softly to his father as the Virginian went to the spring and held his hat, upside-down, beneath the fall. And the youngster ignored him as he moved back along the canyon towards its narrow mouth.

He found the horse grazing on a patch of tough grass at the top of the slope under the towering cliff. It had belonged to Royd Carpenter – a small but strongly built black and white mare. She was on the point of bolting again when Steele appeared. But the smell of the water in his hat held her still for a few moments. Long enough for the Virginian's soft voice, in combination with his un-hurried movements, to calm her.

As she drank, she allowed him to take hold of her bridle. Then submitted to being led back into the canyon.

Steele knew horses. He had been born and bred on one of the largest and best plantations in Virginia, famous throughout the east and south for its livestock. Famous, too, for its owner – Benjamin P. Steele. And for the owner's son, Adam. The respect each held for the other matched only by the regard in which they were held by those who worked for them and those with whom they did business. But then had come the War Between the States.

'Steele, he ain't makin' no sense!' Jack Mason pleaded as the Virginian led the mare to the pool. 'He wants me to blast him!'

The horse began to drink greedily, sucking in the cool water that was now entirely free of the stain of Charlie Risby's blood. Ben Steele had been too old for active combat, but he had played his part – on the opposite side to that for which his son fought. As Steele left the horse and moved to where Jack Mason was comforting his father, he rubbed a thumb over the Colt Hartford's stock plate. Through the thin buck-skin of his glove, he could feel the inscribed lettering: *To Benjamin P. Steele, with gratitude – Abraham Lincoln.*

Steele looked down at the pale face of the critically injured lawman, from which his son had cleaned most of the blood. And it was more obvious than ever that Jack's father would soon be as dead as the Virginian's. But this dying would be with more dignity – if there could be any dignity in death.

The war had been over and some of the scars had begun to heal. The wound which split the Steele father and son was no longer visible. But, on the night Lincoln was shot, Ben Steele was lynched from a beam in a bar-room across the misty street from Ford's Theatre. And Adam Steele had set out on a trail of violent vengeance that had brought him to this blood-stained canyon in the Uinta Mountains. The rich plantation and all it had meant to him was as dead as his father. That was the past. The present and the future demanded constant travel through country such as this: dogged by violence at the dictates of cruel fate and of the forces of law and order which required he pay for the crimes of his vengeance.

'You'd be doing him a favour,' Steele told the youngster,

and the words drew the faintest of smiles from the wounded lawman.

'No!' Jack Mason screamed as the Virginian turned away to go towards his dead horse.

'He's right, son,' the older man groaned. 'I got a lot of lead in my guts. It's like somebody lit a fire down there and now they're stokin' it with irons. I'm gonna die, son. If I was in bed behind the law office in Crest City with the best doc in the country takin' care of me, I'd still snuff it.'

'Shuddup, Pa!' Jack snarled.

Steele took his bedroll from the carcase of the gelding, then unfastened the cinch and struggled to heave off the saddle.

'Listen to me, Jack,' the sheriff urged, his voice weakening with every word he spoke. 'A gut wound is the worst there is. A man has to die with it, but he can last for hours. Back in Crest City, or anyplace else with a doc, there'd be morphine to kill the pain. Out here there ain't no morphine. Only one way to kill the pain.'

'No, Pa!'

There were tears streaming down Jack's cheeks. He raised his father's head and began to kiss the pale, puffy cheeks. The sheriff tried to break the embrace, but he didn't have the strength.

Steele carried his gear over to the pool and the black and white mare submitted meekly to a transfer of saddles.

'The dude's found us a live horse, Pa!' Jack said with sudden excitement as he rested his father's head back on his thigh. 'We can fix up a travois and take you to where there *is* a doc!'

Steele drank his fill from the spring and topped up his two canteens. Then he led the mare over to the Masons.

'Tell him, mister!' the sheriff pleaded, agony etched into every line of his contorted face. 'I ain't got a snowball's chance in hell of travelling half a mile.'

Steele nodded. 'And that half a mile will seem like a hundred to him, kid.'

'Where you goin'?' Jack demanded.

As the Virginian made to swing into the saddle of the mare, Jack Mason snatched for a rifle. Steele's right leg was bent as his foot slid into the stirrup. The split in his pants' seam gaped. His expression hardened almost imperceptibly as his hand streaked away from the saddle horn and delved into the split. It came out even faster. And a smooth flick of the wrist sent the knife spinning.

'No!' the lawman had time to roar. He tried to lift his bulky body and fling it in front of his son. But agony wrenched a scream from his spittle-run lips and weakness flopped him back to the ground.

The knife blade sank home – but not into flesh. Instead, it thudded deep into the ground, dead centre of the Spencer's trigger guard. Its hilt rang against the metal of the guard. Jack Mason gasped and withdrew his hand as if from a striking rattlesnake.

'You've got a quick temper, kid,' Steele warned softly as he stooped, withdrew the knife and picked up the rifle. 'And that can be as fatal as the lead in your father's belly.'

He hurled the rifle ten yards away, returned the knife to the boot sheath, and mounted the mare.

'I still want to know where you're goin', dude!' Jack demanded, his voice betraying a tremor of fear.

'To finish what I started.'

'And leave us here?' There was deep contempt in the youngster's eyes.

'It don't have to be that way,' his father rasped. 'Finish me, Jack. Or get me a gun so I can finish myself. Then ride along with Steele. I did it for a man down in Sonora once. And I'd do it for you.'

'No!'

'It ain't only Hank Jaggs the Tyler bunch has to pay for

now, son. It's Charlie Risby and Quinn Lamont and Dex Spelling and the rest . . . and me.'

'They'll pay, Pa!' his son promised fervantly. 'They'll pay. But first you got to get on the mend!'

The sheriff implored the mounted Steele with his pain-wracked eyes. 'Tell him, mister. Tell him he's wastin' his time.'

Steele pursed his lips. 'It's not that which bothers me, feller. It's the time I'm wasting.'

Now it was the older Mason who expressed contempt. 'So move out then, mister. Unless. . . .' It took Steele a few moments to decide what brand of expression abruptly appeared on the lawman's face. Then he realised what it was – difficult to discern because it was such an unfamiliar set on the features of the tough old man gone soft. Ingratiation. 'Unless you do what I want?'

Jack Mason suddenly sprang erect, uncaring for his father's momentary discomfort as the lawman's head thudded back on to the ground. The tall youngster towered over the injured man, facing Steele as he reached for his empty holsters. The absence of the Colts disconcerted him for only an instant.

'First you'll have to kill me, dude!' he snarled.

Steele shook his head. 'Don't reckon to kill anybody, kid. Unless the Tyler bunch make an issue of it. You riding or stayin'?'

'I'm stayin'!'

This time the Virginian's gesture was affirmative. Then he wheeled the mare.

'But if Pa dies, I'll come after you, dude!' Jack threatened. 'And I'll kill you before I go lookin' for Tyler and his murderin' bastards!'

Steele clucked the horse forward.

'Steele!' the lawman gasped.

The horse was reined to a halt and the rider looked back over the upturned collar of his sheepskin coat.

With enormous effort, the elder Mason managed to raise himself on to one elbow to direct a pleading look towards the mounted man. 'He means it and he'll try to do it. Go easy on him, uh?'

The Virginian pursed his lips. 'His decision, feller.'

'But my fault,' the lawman countered, fresh blood oozing from his stomach wounds after his change of position. 'I never tried to stop him followin' my example.'

'And you're the best example a man ever had, Pa!' Jack exclaimed.

'Not anymore he isn't,' Steele argued, his southern drawl evenly pitched. 'Even if you're tired of living, there are a lot better ways of dying.'

The sheriff fell back into his supine position. His eyes stared unblinkingy up at the darkness pricked by a million pinpoints of starlight. But they did not have the glaze of death and his chest continued to rise and fall shallowly.

'If he dies, *you'll* be the one to follow him, Steele!' the youngster croaked. The tears began to flow again. 'My Pa don't deserve this. He's really somebody.'

The Virginian eyed the dying man with an utterly cold lack of emotion. 'For a while, kid,' he allowed softly. 'But come morning he'll be just another body.'

CHAPTER FIVE

BLACK ROCK was a bigger, better looking town than Crest
City. It was built at a lower altitude, in the western foothills of the Uintas. Wheat and cattle country was spread
out on three sides of it and a tree-fringed lake lay calmly to
the north.

Steele rode into town thirty-six hours after leaving the
dying lawman and his distraught son in the corpse-littered
canyon. He could have reached Black Rock sooner, but he
did not hurry. He had two full eight-hour periods of sleep
and when he moved it was at an easy pace, tracking the
Tyler bunch in the knowledge that the fugitives were not
disposed towards speed.

His second night camp was at the side of a railroad
track which cut diagonally through the foothills, running
south-east to north-west. And, at sun-up, he followed the
track and the sign left by his quarry. Over wild, unused
terrain at first. Then across rolling pasture on which some
good-looking beef was grazing. He smelled smoke and then
began to see neat ranch houses with the hands nearby,
preparing for the day's work. The sun was high enough to
be generating a pleasant warmth as he rode between wheat
fields and emerged on the far side at the edge of town.

The railroad's north-western run ended here, at a stock-
yard and depot dominated by a large painted sign: WEL-
COME TO BLACK ROCK — THE TOWN THAT
GROWS ON THE FINEST WHEAT AND THE BEST
BEEF.

From the depot, two streets formed a large vee, diverging due north and north-west. Both were wide streets flanked by broad sidewalks behind which stood well-built business premises of lumber or brick or a combination of the two. They were single, double and triple storey high. A couple of cross streets joined the main ones. Where the sidewalks ended the main streets became residential, lined by neat houses of many sizes, all of them surrounded by green lawns and white fences.

Black Rock was the kind of town that made a weary and travel-stained newcomer conscious of his dishevelled appearance.

'Hi there, young feller? Wouldn't be lookin' for work, would you?'

It was still not past the breakfast hour and there were few people on Ogden Street, the north bound thoroughfare Steele had chosen to take. Most of those who were in sight were storekeepers opening their doors, polishing display windows and sweeping yesterday's dust off the sidewalks. But the man who addressed the Virginian was a farmer, sitting on a buck-board that stood outside the as yet unopened FEED AND SEED STORE on the corner of a cross street.

'Depends, Steele answered, responding to the pleasant smile which lit the elderly man's freshly shaved and talcumed face.

'On what, young feller?'

'How long my present job lasts.'

There was a three storey building with a BOARDING HOUSE sign above the door on the opposite corner and the Virginian angled the mare towards it.

The farmer bit a chew off a plug of tobacco and nodded. 'All right, young feller. But if you need to earn a buck or two, come on out to my place. Two miles out on the north west trail above the lake. Name of Tucker. Can always use a strong and willin' worker.'

'Farm work ain't exactly your line of work, is it?' another man asked.

Steele had been aware of this man's watchful presence ever since he tugged on the reins to angle the horse across the junction. Aware of him as just a shadowy figure halted in the process of stepping across the threshold of the boarding house doorway. Now, as he spoke and Steele dismounted, the man came out on to the sidewalk. His grey eyes shone as dully as the damp-tarnished star pinned to his shirt front. He was a tall and broad man with a squarish head on which his features seemed to have been chiselled rather than formed by natural development. It was a deeply tanned face, and his eyes and teeth seemed brighter by contrast. He was about forty, dressed in denim pants, a red shirt and a black hat that were all old, but freshly laundered. He looked alert and just a little suspicious.

'If I ever get hungry enough,' Steele replied as he hitched the mare to the rail.

The sheriff nodded and jerked a thumb over his shoulder. 'If you're hungry now, Kate Porter supplies the best breakfast in Black Rock. Best food any time of day, matter of fact.'

'Grateful to you,' the Virginian said.

'Name's Joe South. Welcome to a nice town, Mr. . . . ?'

'Steele.'

'My job to keep it nice, you know what I mean?'

'I reckon.'

The lawman touched the brim of his hat and swung around the corner to head up Ogden Street. Steele had already seen where his office was – at the centre of a brick-built two storey block on the west side, between the Black Rock Bank and the office of *The Sentinel* newspaper. Steele went in through Kate Porter's open door and smelled fresh flowers and wax polish. The hallway of the place was done out like the front parlour of a private house. A chesterfield and two winged chairs, a bureau loaded with three vases of flowers, two wall mirrors in wrought iron frames and a grandfather clock. There was a carpet on the floor and he scattered dust on to it as he took off his hat. The Colt Hartford canted to his shoulder seemed as misplaced as a dime novel carried into a church instead of a Bible.

'My goodness, you're not going to stick us up?'

The elderly, well-rounded woman had entered from a door at the side. The smell of frying bacon and egg wafted into the hallway from behind her. The woman beamed at Steele maternally, then brushed a strand of grey hair off her forehead.

'Not unless that's the only way to get breakfast and a room, ma'am?'

Her smile became even brighter. 'You give me three dollars, Mr Steele and you won't get no trouble from me until this time tomorrow morning.'

She shook her head as Steele expressed surprise. 'I don't have no second-sight. But I'm not yet old enough to have lost my hearing, sir. I heard you and Joe South talking out on the street. You got no need to pay no mind to his tough talk. Leastways, not unless you figure to cause trouble in Black Rock.'

'I'll bear that in mind, ma'am,' the Virginian replied. 'Like a room and chance to clean up before I eat? And take care of my horse.'

The beaming and the pleasant talk was only one facet of the character of Kate Porter. An outstretched hand and a glimmer of avariciousness in her pale blue eyes betrayed the hard businesswoman lurking beneath the motherly softness of her exterior. But the transfer of three dollars from Steele's hip pocket to a pouch in Kate's apron put the shutters up on the less amenable aspect of the woman.

Hatcher's Livery Stables were a block beyond the law office on the other side of the street. On the way down there and back again, Steele saw two hard-eyed deputies on patrol. They moved as a pair, like animals of prey on the prowl, and neither acknowledged the Virginian's casual nod. The first time he saw them, emerging from the Uintas Restaurant, he felt there was something familiar about them. On his way back to the boarding house, minus his horse, they had halted outside the law office and did not go in until he reached the corner. And he pinned down the stray thought that had crossed his mind. Like Joe South, they wore badges of office. Also like the sheriff, they were tall and broad. And had eyes as watchful as those of an eagle after the eggs are laid. One was a couple of years older than South. The other maybe five years younger. Which meant all three lawmen were old enough to know what they wanted and young enough to have a good chance of getting it.

After Steele had cleaned up he discovered that the food at Kate Porter's boarding house was in keeping with his third floor room overlooking the corner – plain but good. But, whereas the room was small, the breakfast he was given amounted to enough for two men. Unaware of when he would have another square meal, the Virginian finished every scrap. And the beaming smile on the again maternal face of Kate indicated she enjoyed watching him demolish the food as much as he relished eating it.

Not so his fellow guests, though. They were a mixed bag of obvious drummers and other transients who did not advertise the reasons for their travel. There were half a dozen men on their own, three married couples – one with two young children – two elderly ladies travelling together and four young men who were friends. Without exception, everyone else taking the first meal of the day in the bright, spacious dining room viewed the newcomer with either distaste for his old, worn and dirty attire or a trace of fear for the way he kept the Colt Hartford always close at hand.

But, by the time he was nearing the end of his breakfast the others became resigned to his presence and talk began to flow freely after a period of low-voiced, desultory conversation interspersed with pregnant pauses. The Virginian learned nothing from it, though. Everyone was waiting either for the ten o'clock train or the stage that was sceduled to connect with it.

However, he realised, as he stood and ambled out of the dining room and across the lobby to step on to the shaded porch, in learning nothing he could be sure of something. The trail he had been following along the railroad indicated that the Tyler gang had come to Black Rock. But, whether they had gone on through or were still in town, it was certain they had not caused any trouble. There was nothing respectable people enjoyed better than talking about the sinful ways of others.

The farmer with the buckboard did not look quite so fresh when Steele saw him for the second time. He was in the process of loading his feed and seed purchases on to his wagon and the exertion and first heat of the sun caused sweat to ooze from every pore. He grimaced his discomfort as the Virginian crossed the street towards him.

'You sure you don't want to work for me, young fellow?' he asked.

Steele leaned his rifle against a wagon wheel and hefted a bulging sack off the sidewalk onto the wagon. 'No charge,' he said. 'You sound as if you ask that question a lot?'

He raised another sack and the farmer took the chance to mop at his shiny brow with a bandana. 'You seen the kind of country this is, young feller. Good and rich. Lots of farms and lots of ranches and plenty of work here in town. But we don't get too many new folks stoppin' by here. On account they got their hearts set on the far West or they want their own piece of land and there just ain't no more hereabouts up for grabs.'

Tucker seemed set to launch into a long and rambling dissertation on the state of the labour market but Steele cut in on him while continuing to load the buckboard.

'Ten men, Mr Tucker. Hit Black Rock yesterday afternoon or last night.'

'What?'

'Did you get a chance to put your proposition to a bunch of fellers who came into town yesterday?'

Ogden Street was a lot busier than when Steele had ridden along it earlier. All the stores were open for business. Saddle horses were hitched to rails and wagons and buggies were rolling in or already parked. People moved on the sidewalks. But the tall sheriff and his two matching deputies stood out in the crowd as they lounged in front of the law office.

'You part of that bunch, young feller?' Tucker asked, abruptly, more than a little nervous.

'Not yet.' Steele loaded the last heavy item and picked up his rifle. There were still a few cardboard cartons stacked on the sidewalk.

Tucker looked at him through narrowed eyes, as if he was short-sighted and anxious to get a lasting impression of the Virginian. Then he shrugged. 'They was in the Trail's End Saloon last night. Ten real mean looking fellers. And real thirsty. Trail's End ain't done such good business since last Thanksgivin' and then it seemed like the whole territory was in there drinkin'.' He grimaced again. 'Coulda been trouble after they was addled by the drink. Wanted girls, but we got us an ordinance against whores in Black Rock. Dancin' girls, likewise. And sure weren't no decent women would go with any of that bunch – and I don't care if they are friends of yours, young feller.'

61

'They've got some money I reckon belongs to me, that's all,' Steele answered with an easy smile that doused the fuse on Tucker's nervousness. 'They move on?'

'Wouldn't know, young feller. Joe South along with Andy Lodge and Curtis Lind calmed that bunch down real fast. Give 'em the choice to take it easy or move on outta Black Rock. But I left to go home to my place soon as the excitement was over.' He sighed and glanced up and down the street. 'This is a fine patch of country to live in, but it's kinda short on excitements.'

'Grateful to you Mr Tucker,' Steele told the man.

'Guess you wouldn't thank me for givin' you advice, young feller?' the farmer suggested, tossing the cartons aboard his wagon. 'But, anyway, I'll tell you that to tangle with that bunch won't get you nothin' but grief.'

He climbed wearily up on to the buckboard seat.

'A man has to take the rough with the smooth,' the Virginian replied.

'And it's only a fool wouldn't know what to take when he's got the choice.' The old eyes narrowed again, for a final close scrutiny of the nondescript good looks and sparsely built frame of the Virginian. 'You don't seem like nobody's fool.'

He released the brake lever, clucked to his two horse team and tugged on the reins to make a U-turn.

'I'll try not to make one of myself,' Steele muttered softly, stepping back into the shade of the gallery above the feed and seed store.

His dark eyes roved the street, flicking over faces and places. But his casual attitude belied the thought processes of his mind. From what he knew of the Tyler gang, they took what they wanted. That made them the kind of men who, if their desires were not satisfied, would react violently in their dissatisfaction. No matter how capable South,

Lodge and Lind were as law officers, the Tyler bunch were unlikely to back down from them – unless they had a good and selfish reason for doing so.

Thus, behind his easy stance and indifferent expression, Steele was searching for what that reason could be. And, when he saw a familiar face, he did not betray his success by even the blinking of an eyelid. It was an ugly face, once seen never forgotten. Painfully thin, with sunken cheeks and small eyes in the pits of deep sockets. A face Steele had first seen above a rifle that blasted death from over the grassy knoll in the canyon where so many men had become corpses. Now he saw the frame beneath the face - long and sparsely fleshed, attired in a shirt, pants and boots as black as his high-crowned, narrow-brimmed hat. The drabness of the garb relieved only by the dangerous glint of polished bullets slotted around the length of the man's gunbelt.

The only member of the Tyler gang Steele was able to recognise sat astride a strong-looking black mare hitched to the rail in front of the Black Rock Bank. He was not alone. Another man astride a less distinguished-looking brown gelding was next to him and the two were talking. The second man was shorter and a lot fatter, with dark-skinned features that were a match for the Mexican sombrero he wore. A riderless saddle horse was also hitched to the bank's rail.

In watching the two men, the Virginian was also able to see the farmer, Tucker. The elderly man had reined his team to a halt on a signal from Joe South and the sheriff and his two deputies had crossed the street to talk with Tucker. The answers which South got to his questions caused all three lawmen to glance along the street and then fix Steele with puzzled stares.

Tucker was waved on his way and as he drove out beyond the business area of town, his buckboard was passed by the incoming stage. The coach was early and from far to the south east came the plaintive wail of a train whistle, like a plea for patience.

The rich-looking bank with two bank robbers waiting outside spelled trouble. But not immediately, for eight of the Tyler gang were absent from the scene – or perhaps only seven if the spare horse belonged to one of them. So Steele recommenced his surveillance of the entire length of Ogden Street instead of just the area immediately around the bank.

But he no longer had a reference by which to judge the faces, and the task was suddenly made harder by a quickening of the slow pace of morning life in Black Rock. The appearance of the stage and the advance notice that the train was due had caused a flurry of activity. For awhile, it seemed that only Steele, the trio of lawmen and the two horsemen outside the bank were not hurrying towards the depot where the stage had already halted and where preparations were underway for the arrival of the train.

The horsemen remained where they were; South and his deputies ambled back towards the law office immediately next door to the bank, and Steele began to stroll in the direction of the bank. Whether or not the thin man and the Mexican were recognised as two of last night's troublemakers, South and the deputies ignored them and concentrated on the loose-limbed approach of Steele.

As he stepped down off the sidewalk to cross the junction of the main and side streets, the Virginian saw that a great many other people were uninterested in the stage and the train. As the locomotive hauled its cars to a clattering halt and hissed a powerful sigh of steamy relief, the majority of Black Rock continued about its daily business, ignoring the hustle and bustle down at the depot.

The sun beat down and small puffs of dust rose from under Steele's feet. Everybody except the lawmen appeared at ease and, on the surface, the two mounted men seemed as relaxed as only the totally guiltless have a right to be.

'You'll be in to lunch, I hope, Mr Steele?'

This was called by Kate Porter, who stepped down from the sidewalk in front of a grocery store and raised a parasol as she started across the street. A clerk from the store was immediately behind her, weighed down by two overloaded baskets of cartons and cans.

'Man would be a fool to miss out on a chance to eat at your place, ma'am,' Steele replied, touching the brim of his hat with his free hand.

The gloved thumb of his other hand cocked the hammer of the Colt Hartford as the thin man and the Mexican turned in their saddles to glance towards him. But their expressions of indifference did not change: both of them had failed to carry an impression of him out of the night darkened canyon.

'I hope you ate a hearty breakfast, Steele! Pa died!'

The two members of the Tyler gang were no longer disinterested. And the watchful, impassive gazes of South, Lodge and Lind abruptly flicked away from Steele. The Virginian halted and, as the dust settled around him, the heat of the sun seemed suddenly more intense.

Jack Mason must have seen him from the depot. Without a horse, he would have reached Black Rock by train. The stage had rolled into town from the wrong direction. And, with his quarry spotted, he had made good time approaching it. But without drawing attention to himself until he spat the hate-dripping words at Steele.

'How long did it take?' the Virginian asked, turning just his head to look towards the new orphan.

He was ten yards away and over on the right, diagonally across the street from Steele.

'Two hours!' He was dirty and unshaven. From the look

of his eyes, he had not slept since the last time Steele saw him. He seemed to have doubled in age over the intervening hours. But the dull, heavy-lidded eyes did not blink against the strong sunlight. And the hands hanging close to the ivory butts of the matched Colts were rock still. 'And every minute it got worse for him.'

'Son!' Joe South said, his voice ringing out loud and clear and emotionless. 'Anyone shoots off a gun in Black Rock, he goes to gaol. He kills anyone with the gun, he gets hung.'

Steele turned to face the front again at the sound of the sheriff's voice. And he was in time to see a man stroll out of the bank's open doorway and look questioningly at the two mounted men before swinging into the saddle of the third horse. He was about forty, which was around the same age as the others. A stocky man with a bullet head and a face that had taken a lot of beatings in a lot of brawls, or suffered terribly as the result of one. The flesh was a mass of scar tissue and misshapen planes. But the brightness of his light eyes seemed to warn that the battering had not dulled the sharp edges of his brain.

'But he might have lived if he'd had the hope he was gonna be helped!' Jack Mason went on, totally ignoring the sheriff's threat. 'You didn't let him have that, Steele. So, when he died, I put him and the others in the cave and then I came to do what I said I would.'

'You better listen to me, son!' Joe South barked. And this time there was a menacing tone to power the words. He took a step forward and Lind and Lodge moved up on either side of him. All three lawmen adopted a similar stance to Mason. But the deputies were nervous. They flexed their fingers and their eyes darted constantly between the street and their boss.

'I'd advise you to do just that, young man!' Kate Porter said.

66

The grocery store clerk had managed to back off onto the relative safety of the sidewalk. But the elderly woman held her ground and her voice was as calm as her expression.

'Turn around, you pint-sized dude bastard!' the revenge-bent youngster demanded. 'Turn around or you'll get it like a thousand other Johnnie Rebs.'

'*Si!*' the mounted Mexican exclaimed gleefully. 'But many more than one thousand die with bullet in back when running from victorious Yankees!'

'Keep it down, Raul!' the bright-eyed man hissed. 'We ain't no part of this!'

He reached forward to unhitch his reins from the rail. The gaunt-faced man did likewise, but the Mexican was reluctant to leave the scene of a possible shoot-out.

Mason's taunt did not strike home. The Virginian acknowledged many faults in his character, but a quick temper was no longer one of them. Had he not been able to conquer this trait, he would have died long ago: forced into thoughtless action which would have been taken advantage of by a cooler adversary. And, as a former soldier in a defeated army moving across a country where the war was still contested verbally, he had learned to live with such insults. The alternative was to die.

Not that he ever allowed them to pass without retaliation. An inability to turn the other cheek was a fault he had never tried to bury in the past. He merely weighed up his choice of actions before embarking upon one of them. He turned just his head again, his dark eyes as cold as the workings of his mind behind them.

'You had the same warnin' I gave the kid, Steele!' Joe South barked. 'So both of you – ditch the guns.'

'Remember the job we started out to do, feller,' Steele said.

'Don't call me a kid!' Mason snarled. The demand was

directed at Joe South, but the youngster did not make the mistake of taking his gaze away from Steele.

'We've got a good chance of doing that job here,' Steele continued.

'Don't you talk back to Mr South, *kid!*' Curtis Lind yelled.

'Talk's done!' Mason countered.

'Listen – ' Kate Porter started, pushing out a foot to take a long stride. But she was at least three yards out of the line of fire.

Mason drew. The same fast, double-handed snatch and level of the matching Colts Steele had witnessed twice already. But, this time, he was in no position merely to stand and watch. He held still only until Mason's hands fisted around the revolver butts. Then he flicked his right wrist to swing down the rifle. His left hand came up and across to accept the barrel into the gloved palm.

'Crazy kid!' South roared.

Steele threw himself to the side then, as he heard more guns snatched from holsters and cocked.

It was the Colt Hartford which cracked first. A woman's scream made a higher pitched sound. Kate Porter did not vent it. Steele caught a fleeting glimpse of her – corkscrewing to the ground with her eyes closing as she fainted. In the same instant, he saw blood spouting from Mason's upper left arm. The youngster started to turn, his wounded arm flapping down and the gun falling from it, unfired.

But, as Steele had guessed, Mason had a vast storehouse of willpower to call on. Hatred fuelled his determination and he froze in the turn and squeezed the trigger of his second gun. The bullet cracked across the acute angle of the Virginian's falling frame. The lawmen yelled their alarm and scattered. Glass shattered from a bank window. The three horses snorted and one started to rear.

Steele slammed into the ground and fired a second shot.

Mason screamed. But not with pain. The bullet tore through the leather of his right boot, smashed between two of his toes and gouged a bloody furrow along the sole and heel of his foot. It was frustration from the missed shot and fear of Steele's rifle that powered the scream from his gaping mouth. Still turned sideways on to Steele, Mason toppled as his right leg collapsed under him.

He struggled to get his Colt to the aim, but his fall was fast and uncontrolled. And, as the scream died on his lips, the expression on his face became totally one of fear. For the Virginian had his feet beneath him now and was in a tense crouch, with the stock of the rifle into his shoulder and his eye behind the backsight. The Colt Hartford's muzzle drew a fixed bead on Mason's chest as the youngster completed his fall. The slightest pressure of the gloved finger around the trigger would have crashed a .44 calibre bullet into Mason's heart.

Despite pain and fear, the youngster snatched for a last chance at survival. He hurled the revolver away from him. It bounced against Kate Porter's fallen parasol and dropped into the dust of the street.

'Steele!' Joe South roared.

The Virginian sensed at least one gun levelled at his back. A babble of conversation erupted, coming from every side. Sweat coursed down his forehead, jaw and neck. But Mason's fear-contorted features were a great deal wetter. He was half raised off his side by his good arm. Blood from his two wounds dripped into the dust and the ground drank it with parched greed.

'Let's move!' This from the bright-eyed man.

As hooves clopped on the sun-baked street, Steele straightened and tipped the rifle back to his shoulder. But the hammer was still cocked. Mason had shot off his mouth about burying more than just his father in a cave. And this had tripped a warning bell in the mind of at least one of the trio of mounted men. The voice of the one with bright eyes had rang with an urgent tone.

'So you're too friggin' good for me, dude!' Mason yelled, his voice cutting across a long sigh rasping from Joe South's mouth. 'But you ain't better than the whole Tyler bunch!'

'Move, I said!' the bright-eyed bank robber roared.

All three horses snorted their pain as spurred heels crashed into their flesh. The animals lunged from an easy walk into the full gallop.

'What the hell?' Lodge bellowed.

It was Steele's action which drew the exclaimation. For the Virginian pivoted on toe and heel, the rifle whipping down and then carried high, to thud the stock into his shoulder.

'No more!' a woman shrieked.

'Steele!' the sheriff snarled.

He squeezed off a shot, but it was meant only as a warning. The bullet went high and wide, cracking across the roof of Hatcher's Livery Stables. The three horsemen all reacted to the shot. The thin man and the Mexican both leaned forward, stooping low in their saddles. The one with bright eyes drew a revolver and started to turn. As his face swung into view, the light-coloured eyes clearly visible through the dust rising from under the galloping hooves, Steele's rifle exploded for a fourth time. The bullet entered through the jaw, its upward trajectory taking it into and out of the tongue and then dictated a course through the back of the throat. It penetrated the rear of the skull, but lodged there. Thus, there was only the entry wound to torrent liquid crimson as the man spun off his horse and crashed to the ground. The horse kept on running. Its former rider lay utterly still. The thin man and the Mexican went into a tight turn – plunging out of sight around the corner of the northern cross street.

The Virginian betrayed his discontent by a grunt that was inaudible to all ears save his own. He canted the rifle back to his shoulder and eased the hammer to the rest. The beat of hooves faded into the distance. Jack Mason sobbed and Kate Porter groaned her intention to return to consciousness.

'We gonna arrest him, Joe?' Lind asked.

'Or kill him if he don't surrender,' the sheriff acknowledged.

The Virginian glanced towards the three lawmen and saw that they all had revolvers aimed at him. Then he nodded along the street to where a group of curious people had closed in around the corpse of the once bright-eyed man.

'That's one of ten fellers who robbed a bank in Crest City and murdered the manager,' he said.

The two deputies expressed tacit interest with an undertone of concern. The sheriff spat.

'And the kid?'

Mason was in too much pain to respond to the word he considered an insult. And he was lost to sight in the crowd that surrounded him and Kate Porter.

'All that's left of the Crest City posse that came after the Tyler bunch.'

Joe South spat again. 'And the way you been blastin' at both sides, seems you're piggy in the middle, uh?'

The Virginian showed the faintest of smiles as he shook his head. 'I don't reckon I'm a pig, feller,' he replied evenly. 'I'm only in for ten cents on the dollar.'

CHAPTER SIX

SHERIFF South had seen the way Steele always had the Colt Hartford within easy reach and he sensed that this was not entirely for protection. So he did not broach the subject of the rifle's surrender. Lodge and Lind followed his example in holstering their guns and continued to show expressions which were intrigued and anxious in equal parts. No further mention was made of arresting Steele, but from both the Virginian and the sheriff there seemed a tacit acceptance of their positions. Steele had agreed to co-operate providing South did not push too hard.

And it was obviously this unspoken agreement which disturbed the two deputies as they were assigned their duties – Lind to check over and take care of the corpse and Lodge to question Mason after the wounded youngster had been carried into the doctor's office.

The group of bystanders – which had been swelled to a large crowd as people came running, attracted by the shots – also expressed uncomprehending curiosity at Joe South's lack of decisive action. But, in no fear of losing their jobs, they were able to voice their feelings.

'Well, ain't you gonna take away his rifle, Joe?' a man asked.

'He just gunned down two men, sheriff. Right here on Ogden Street in Black Rock.' This from an attractive young woman. She sounded as if she could not believe the evidence of her own eyes.

'And for money, from what he said,' added a man at the woman's side.

'He's not the sort I want staying at my place,' a pale-faced, ramrod-stiff Kate Porter exclaimed, shaking off the support of two elderly men. Her blue eyes fixed Steele with an accusing stare. 'Whatever you took into my house will be outside the front door just as soon as I get back!'

As the volume of noise rose, so each voice cut across another and none could be heard clearly. Steele remained in a casual attitude, his expression neutral. But the verbal onslaught got to the sheriff, who reddened and grew tense.

'Go about your business!' he suddenly roared. It brought silence to the street and he lowered his voice. 'And let the law attend to what it has to do.' His dull grey eyes raked the faces of the crowd and he nodded his satisfaction with what he had achieved. Then he jerked a thumb over his shoulder as he looked at the Virginian. 'You want to step inside and explain yourself, Steele?'

There was no visible or audible threat from South, but neither was he making a request.

Steele showed a wry smile as he started forward. He glanced up at the sky and then around at the faces in the crowd. 'It is getting a little heated out here,' he said softly.

'On your way, I told you!' the lawman barked as Steele stepped up on to the sidewalk to go behind him, and only a handful of the bystanders began to move.

'Five minutes to stage time!' a man yelled from down in front of the railroad depot. And the locomotive engineer sounded his whistle in a strident announcement that the train was also getting ready to pull out. The break-up of the crowd was abruptly accelerated.

Joe South executed another nod and smiled with his mouth as he spun around. But the smile froze on his lips when he saw that Steele was going into the bank instead of the law office.

'Like to talk to you about that feller I just killed,' the Virginian said to the man who backed off from him, nervously retreating into the bank.

He was a man of about fifty: no taller than five feet with a round, pale face and a drooping belly that seemed to start beneath his series of double chins. Despite the heat, he was dressed in a city suit with a high-collared shirt and a neatly-fastened necktie. A green eyeshade jutted out from the front of his bald pate and rimless spectacles magnified his green eyes. His pudgy hands twitched and he licked dry lips as Steele spoke to him.

'Hey, you!' South yelled, feet thudding on the sidewalk.

The bank clerk whirled and half ran, half waddled through a gap in the end of the counter. He kicked the gate closed and slammed down the hinged section of top. As if the counter was a barricade against everything that could hurt him, he breathed a deep sigh of relief.

Steele glanced around the red brick walls hung with coloured prints and eyed the polished wood furnishings. The short, fat man was the only employee on duty and there were no customers. As the sheriff stepped heavily across the threshold, the clerk gained his proper work place, locking himself into a gilt-barred teller's cage. The security of the bars enabled him to smile and he dropped five years in age.

'Yes, sir, what can I do for you?' he asked. His voice was high-pitched – almost girlish. It was his natural tone, for he was no longer afraid.

'I mean my office, Steele!' Joe South growled. 'And you know it.'

'Be there in a minute,' the Virginian drawled and made a further surveillance of the rich-looking interior of the bank. This time, beyond the counter which ran across the big room. There were three tellers' cages. Behind these there was an office with a polished door bearing a legend in gold block capitals: *Cedric Harvey, President.* And the vault, its smooth concrete facing interrupted only by the metal door which shone with a dull sheen.

'I told you, Mr Rhodes,' Steele said, reading the clerk's name off a pasteboard sign in front of the man.

'I am not at liberty to discuss the bank's clients,' Rhodes replied.

'And your liberty is in the balance, mister!' the sheriff barked, moving into the Virginian's range of vision. 'You'll sure as hell lose it if you don't have a good explanation of what just happened out there.'

'Dead man was a client?'

Rhodes sucked the inside of his flabby cheek. 'He intended to be. Stopped by to enquire the minimum deposit we accept to open an account.' The eyes behind the lenses became a little scornful. 'He was most polite.'

'That was all?'

Rhodes shot a questioning glance at the sheriff. South expelled another sigh.

'This guy seems big for his boots, Alvin,' the lawman said evenly. 'But maybe he ain't too big for them.'

'You mean I should tell him, Mr South?'

'You'll be tellin' me too, Alvin. And they're the same questions I'd be askin' you later anyway.'

Alvin Rhodes shrugged and looked at the sheriff as he spoke. 'He asked about the investment facilities we have. And about trust funds for his two children. I went into a great deal of detail for him. He was really most polite.'

'Anythin' else, Steele?' South growled.

'Then he left?' Steele to Rhodes.

'Then he left.' Rhodes to South.

'That's it.' Steele to South.

It was the Virginian who turned first, and led the way

out of the bank. The sheriff trailed him. The few hardline rubbernecks still loitering outside the bank expressed a degree of satisfaction at this arrangement.

'You think I should go get Mr Harvey?' Rhodes called.

'Do whatever you want, Alvin,' South responded unhelpfully.

'Just don't stand in front of the vault when the Tyler bunch come for the money,' Steele muttered, only loud enough for South to hear.

Then he turned into the law office. Andy Lodge was hurrying towards the same objective from one end of the street. Curtis Lind was taking his time approaching it from the other end. South dropped into a swivel chair behind one of the two desks in the clean and uncluttered law office. He pushed his hat on to the back of his head and gestured ungraciously for Steele to sit in the rigid chair before the desk.

'All right, mister,' he rasped. 'You've made your point. You're a hard-nosed killer who gets what he wants come hell or high water. Now let me make my position clear. I don't like killers or killin' in any way, shape or form. Which was why I didn't put on the pressure out in the street awhile back. You wouldn't get took without a fight. And there were a lot of innocent folk out there. Some of them coulda got hurt.'

Heavy footfalls sounded on the sidewalk, then clumped into the office.

'Joe, the kid reckons this guy is a –'

'Hold it, Andy!' South cut in on Lodge's breathless announcement. Then, 'Cover him!'

Steele's facial muscles tightened, and this was his sole visible reaction to the order and the actions that followed it. South's right hand was suddenly on the desk top, fisted around the butt of a Colt aimed at Steele's chest. A grunt and some other sounds from behind him announced that

76

the out of breath deputy was happy to have one of his own guns out and aimed.

'Me and my deputies get paid for takin' risks, Steele,' the sheriff said, and this time the smile reached all the way from his mouth to his eyes and back again. 'So you just slide that rifle onto this desk – stock towards me.'

Deep inside, the Virginian was as tense as his expression. But only for a moment, as an initial reaction to being caught yet again in the centre of a cross-fire situation. Then he relaxed and complied with the order. This time he was totally trapped. Snap shots were not going to save him, as they had done in the canyon and out on Ogden Street.

'You're overpaid, feller,' Steele said softly as South gripped the Colt Hartford with his free hand and dragged it across the desk. He lowered it gently to the floor. 'This play is about as risky as playing poker with a blind man.'

The footfalls of Curtis Lind sounded in the office. They halted abruptly and then came another sound – as he drew his gun from its holster.

'About time, Joe!' the newcomer said, with a note of triumph in his voice.

South picked up on the comment but ignored the speaker as he concentrated his attention on the Virginian. 'Time was always on our side, Steele. And you know the score when it's like that. You bide your time until the right opportunity turns up. You get to live longer that way.'

Steele nodded his agreement and now the tension went out of his expression. He leaned back on the chair and crossed his legs. 'The cemetaries are crowded with over-eager heroes, feller. You biding your time with the Tyler bunch, too?'

This time it was Steele's comment which South ignored. But he didn't break his concentration on the Virginian as he asked a question of Lodge. 'What's the kid's version, Andy?'

77

'Name of Mason, Joe,' came the eager reply. 'Son of the sheriff of Crest City . . .'

Lodge had recovered from the exertion of his fast return to the law office. But he still sounded a little breathless – with excitement – as he reported what he had learned from Jack Mason. It was accurate in every detail, until Lodge left a pregnant pause and South demanded:

'Is that it, Andy?'

'No, Joe. Kid reckons he overheard Steele talking to another guy in the posse. Seems Steele don't want just the reward. Figures to take the whole bundle that the Tyler bunch has got left. Wanted this other guy to help if the posse tried to stop it happening.'

'That right, mister?' South asked the Virginian.

Steele pursed his lips. 'Mason told it straight up until that last part.'

The lawman grimaced. 'Even about you ridin' off and leavin' his old man to die?'

'He was dead already,' Steele answered. 'He just wouldn't stop breathing. First he asked his boy to kill him. Then me. But I reckoned it was a family matter.'

South kept the grimace in place. 'What about the other guy he blasted, Curtis?'

'Dead before he hit the street, looks like, Joe,' Lind replied grimly. 'Half what he had in his head run out through his mouth.'

'What was in his pockets?' South snapped.

'No identification, Joe,' Lind said hurriedly. 'Money is all. Better than nine hundred dollars. Eighty three dollars better.'

South greeted the news of the high amount as stoically as Steele.

'Would have been less, I reckon,' the Virginian commented. 'If there wasn't an ordinance against cat houses in Black Rock.'

The sheriff sighed. 'I oughta lock you up in a cell back there, Steele,' he growled, jerking a thumb over his shoulder to indicate an archway giving onto the rear of the law office. 'And I oughta send word up to Crest City for them to take you off my hands.'

'But ain't we gonna do just that, Joe?' Lind asked, surprised.

South holstered his gun and broke his concentrated gaze at Steele for the first time. He worked some saliva up into his mouth and aimed it with the skill of long practise at a spittoon in a corner of the office. 'The kid's got a grudge. On account of his old man snuffin' it and on account he's gotta couple of bullet holes in him. Only natural he's sore.'

It wasn't meant as a joke and nobody laughed at it. Certainly not South, who looked as if he was sucking on something that tasted sour.

'But why we gotta believe Steele instead of him, Joe?' Lodge wanted to know. 'It's one guy's word against another. One the son of a sheriff and the other a bounty hunter more or less.'

The tall lawman pressed his hands hard against the desk top to lever himself up out of the chair. He came around from behind it and crossed to the door. Steele turned on his chair to watch South and saw the two deputies holster their Colts in response to a gesture from the sheriff. Then South stood at the door, sideways on, like an usher. He jerked a thumb out of the shaded office towards the sun bright street.

'Get your rifle and get outta here, Steele. And I just don't mean outta the law office. I mean outta town. You're gunnin' for Olney Tyler and his boys. They ain't in Black Rock.'

Steele stood, leaned over the desk to get the Colt Hartford, and canted it to his shoulder. 'One of them is, feller,' he reminded.

South blinked back the memory of the dead man. 'You bring the money, Curtis?' he asked. 'The nine hundred and eighty three dollars?'

Lind delved under his shirt and brought out the bankroll he had taken from the corpse. He extended it towards South, who accepted it in a meaty hand.

'I'm holdin' this roll,' South said evenly. 'And I'll get a message up to Crest City. If I get the right kinda answer, your ten per cent will be waitin' here for you.'

Steele considered the proposition for long moments, then nodded. 'On one condition, sheriff.'

'What's that?'

'You don't put it in the bank vault.'

South's grin had a taunting quality. 'You havin' second thoughts, Steele? You figure there's a chance that this is the only loot you're gonna get back from the Tyler gang?'

'Maybe,' Steele allowed. 'But I'm like you, feller. I don't like to take risks when they're not necessary. Maybe the man who cased the bank is dead, but I still reckon the vault is a risky place to keep anything valuable for a while.'

'Beat it, Steele.'

The Virginian moved across the office and stepped out onto the sidewalk. South eyed his progress impassively. The two deputies were held midway between disappointment and disgust. Outside, many eyes cast surreptitious glances towards the slightly built Virginian. But there were no protests voiced. South's demand for the law to be allowed to take care of its own business had apparently been met.

Although the morning was now well advanced, Black Rock was quieter and less busy than it had been earlier. Both the train and the stage had pulled out and, with their departure, a brand of baleful tranquility had descended upon the town. Almost as if the dead bank robber had been a respected citizen of Black Rock whose passing was being mourned. But there was no bell tolling, as there had been in Crest City for Hank Jaggs.

Steele went first down to Kate Porter's boarding house on the corner of Ogden and the cross street. The woman's threat had not been an idle one. His bedroll and saddle-bags had been tossed out into the dust of the street. As he picked up the gear, the blanket and leather were hot to the touch from being so long under the blazing sun. When he went into the rich-smelling atmosphere of Hatcher's Livery Stables, the elderly owner was just completing the chore of saddling the black and white mare. His leathery features expressed apology and anxiety.

'Mr Lodge was just over,' he explained. 'Said you was leavin' and I was to saddle up your horse.'

'The law gives a comprehensive service in this town,' Steele said evenly, checking the tension of the cinch and finding it was perfect.

'Joe South's a good man and a fine peace officer,' Hatcher answered, not heated. 'Utah Territory is mostly Mormon country. But the town of Black Rock was here before them religious adulterers ever got run outta the east. Tried to move in on us and it was Joe who led the fight against them. A lot younger then, and he wasn't sheriff. But we sure give him the office fast. And he's kept trouble outta town ever since.'

'Until last night,' Steele said evenly, taking a long time to fix on his bedroll. The stooped old man with a twisted right arm was obviously anxious to talk. And Steele was ready to listen if the topic was the one that interested him.

'Last night?' Hatcher squinted in puzzlement.

'The Tyler gang rode in.'

The old man made a sound of disgust. 'And out again, fast. They didn't make no trouble, 'cause Joe South didn't give them no chance.'

'You in the saloon, feller?' What did he tell them?'

'Don't know that,' Hatcher admitted, and it was obvious he resented the lack of knowledge. 'Joe and his deputies cleared the saloon of everyone 'ceptin' the strangers. Only know they was on their horses and ridin' outta Black Rock damn lot faster than they rode in.'

'Seems like he's a real ball of fire,' Steele mused as he led the mare towards the open double doors of the stables.

'He gets things done, sure enough,' Hatcher responded. 'Stops trouble before it has a chance to start.' He made the sound of disgust again. 'Most of the time, anyway. Your run-in with them other two guys took him unawares, I guess.'

'There wasn't the time to send out any printed invitations to the event,' Steele answered wryly.

Outside, he swung up into the saddle and swept his gaze from one end of Ogden Street to the other. There were even less people in sight than a few minutes earlier. Those that were on the street pointedly avoided looking at the Virginian. But he sensed countless pairs of eyes fixed upon him.

He clucked the mare forward, pulling gently on the reins to steer her across the street on a diagonal line towards the corner where the thin man and the Mexican had ridden out of sight. Then two stirs of movement caught his attention. Close at hand, a man rode out of the alley at the end of the block comprising the bank and the law and newspaper offices. It was the grim-faced Curtis Lind astride a good-looking tan gelding. Four canteens were hung from the saddlehorn and the saddle-bags were fat with supplies for a long ride.

'He's riding to Crest City, Steele!' the sheriff called from the shadows beyond the law office doorway. 'This is other folks' trouble and we want no part of it.'

'I reckon I can understand that, feller,' the Virginian

82

called in reply. 'How many stages hit Black Rock every day?'

'One. Why?' South was less gruff. He was curious.

'Then I reckon you got some trouble of your own,' Steele told him, reining the mare to a halt and pointing to the north.

Out beyond the facing rows of houses, where the street became an open trail, there was grassland all the way to the southern shore of the big lake. Spreading away from the eastern shore there was a broad expanse of timber. The trail plunged through the trees and it was at this point that the second flurry of movement had attracted Steele's attention. When he had first seen the large cloud of dust billow from where the trail disappeared into the timber, there had been no way of knowing exactly what caused it. But now, as the sound of hectic progress reached his ears, he got more than a glimpse of the stage and its four-horse team hurtling towards Black Rock.

'It's the stage comin' back, Joe!' Lind yelled.

But South did not need the information. The sheriff was just one of a crowd who had spilled out on to the street when the sound of beating hooves and rattling wheels assaulted the ears of the town.

'And comin' like the Devil himself is after it!' the aged Hatcher yelled.

Dust continued to shroud the racing stage, spewed up from under the pumping hooves and spinning wheels. But it was obvious that the team was not in an uncontrolled bolt. The horses were steered skilfully around the trail's curves and, even as the more anxious people in the crowd leapt for the safety of the sidewalk, the dust-veiled driver started to slow the flat out gallop.

The speed had been halved by the time the stage rolled between the neat houses. And then the sweat-lathered animals walked the final few yards until they were brought

83

to a halt in front of the crowd. The driver was a stockily built man in his mid-forties with the burnished and crinkled face of one who has spent more time out of doors than in. A man who had seen a lot and done a lot in his life. But the horror that contorted his face was a tacit statement that nothing like today had ever happened to him before.

'What is it, Erle?' Hatcher yelled. 'You look like you –'

'Inside the friggin' stage!' the driver said, his voice a snarl. 'Every friggin' last one of them! Both friggin' barrels of a friggin' shotgun! Then rifles. Friggin' rifles. Just pour-ed friggin' lead into them like they was slaughterin' friggin' animals. Men, women and kids. And friggin' me couldn't do friggin' nothin' 'cept sit up here and friggin' pray.'

'Oh, my God!' Curtis Lind gasped, as he rode his geld-ing to the side of the stage and peered inside. The naturally hard set of his features softened dramatically and every trace of colour left his skin.

The Virginian moved his horse in close to the other side of the stage. And he recalled how, a few days ago, he had reflected on the absence of violence from his life over the past weeks. The smile of fate had been a false one. Behind it, death had been stockpiled. First the water-bloated body of Hank Jaggs. Next the massacre in the canyon. Then the blasting guns on Black Rock's main street. Now the charnel house on wheels that the sweating team had dragged into town.

There had been eight passengers aboard the stage and Steele recognised just one face – the woman who had been having breakfast with her husband and two children at the boarding house a few hours earlier. Perhaps he would recognise others, once the bodies were taken out of the coach and cleaned of the great splashes of drying blood that daubed their faces and clothing.

Two of them would not be identified from their faces,

even by their nearest and dearest. For shotgun charges at close range had blasted the flesh-formed features off their skulls. One a man and the other a woman. They had died as they sat, in corner seats facing each other. And they had apparantly been the first to be blasted into eternity. The rest of the passengers had been panicked into escape attempts by the shotgun blasts: and some had not died quickly. Bodies were slumped across the seats, crumpled on the floor or folded on top of other bodies. Crimson-run holes pocked faces, torsoes and limbs. The faces which could be seen expressed naked terror and mind-shattering agony.

The carnage toppled the deputy off his horse in a total faint and he was in danger of being trampled as the towns-people crowded in close to the stage to peer inside. Steele backed off his horse to give the curious room on his side of the coach.

'Didn't take a friggin' cent off any of us!' Erle went on. 'Just stopped the friggin' stage, came in close and started blastin' with their friggin' guns.'

He was shouting now, to be heard above the gasps, the groans and shocked voices of the crowd. Those at the rear tried to force a way to the front, eager to experience the same degree of horror as everyone else.

'Quiet!' South yelled. And, when the order was not instantly obeyed, he drew both his handguns and exploded them into the sky. Then: 'Who, Erle? Who did it? Why'd they do it?'

The silence was absolute as every pair of eyes swung to the trembling stage driver. Up until now he had been staring straight ahead, as if struggling to recall the story he had committed to an unreliable memory. But now he sought out and found the tall lawman, his eyes having difficulty in focusing.

He shook his head. 'They didn't say who they was, Mr

South.' He spoke quietly and without profanity now. 'But they give me a message for you. They said that what's aboard the stage is just a sample. They said you shouldn't have killed Pete Salter. They said they're comin' to town and they want you to hand over every cent in Black Rock. Not only what's in the bank, Mr South. Every cent that all the folks have got.' He turned around and stared down at the roof of his stage. 'And if they don't get what they want, this is just a sample of what'll happen.'

'When, Erle?' South asked grimly. 'When are they comin'?'

'Didn't say exactly, Mr South. Just said they'd be here soon. But they said you'd know when they got here.'

Horror became fear on many of the faces. It was a smell on Ogden Street, released by the sweat glands of the tightly packed bystanders. South, still holding his Colts which were now pointed at the ground, expressed confused anxiety for long moments. In the doorway of the law office, Andy Lodge watched closely, ready to adopt whatever attitude the sheriff elected. Curtis Lind groaned back to consciousness among the feet of the crowd.

'You can handle it, Joe!' Hatcher urged, growing two inches as he straightened the stoop out of his shoulders. 'You done it before, with us behind you.'

'Damn right!' the voice of Kate Porter called from the centre of the crowd. 'You kept them lust-filled Mormon people out of Black Rock. Ain't a man – nor woman too – won't back you in fightin' off these murderin' sonsof-bitches!'

The babble of conversation that followed these comments had a confident tone. The sun was bright and the town was secure. The stage passengers had not been dead long enough to start stinking yet.

The Virginian wheeled his horse and moved around the rear of the crowd towards the uncluttered street.

86

'Except for one man, it seems!' Kate yelled.

Steele sensed all eyes swing towards him. His back was towards them and the contempt and hatred directed at him seemed to have a physical force, urging him on his way.

'Nothin' to worry about, folks!' Lodge yelled, his tone heavy with scorn. 'He figures to ride out alone and save the town.' His spit into the dust was very loud. 'He ain't very big, but he sure is mighty crazy!'

There was a low mumbling of agreement with the deputy's opinion. Then a rifle shot.

Steele was riding between the first pair of private residences. The bullet cracked from an upstairs window of the house on the right. It took the black and white mare cleanly in the right eye and the animal died on its feet. An instant later, as a torrent of blood fountained from the wound, the horses's forelegs jack-knifed. Steele, tight-lipped and with his narrow eyes raking the street to locate the sniper, reached for the Colt Hartford in the boot. But the forward cant and then the roll of the dead animal hurled him from the saddle. He hit the ground with a shoulder and snatched his legs from under the falling weight of the horse. The rifle cracked again and dust spurted into his grimacing face as the bullet drilled into the ground.

'Freeze, dude!' Jack Mason snarled. 'Or you're as dead as my Pa!'

Mason's face, pale and drawn, was framed by the bed-room window of the house. Lace curtains were draped over his shoulders. The barrel of a Winchester rifle was angled downwards from between the same curtains. It was as unmoving as the trunk of the live oak tree growing on one side of the garden in front of the house. On the tree trunk was a shingle lettered with the name of Dr. Silas Grant.

Steele flicked his gaze towards his own rifle. He had to look along the length of his body and then across the carcase of the horse. Which was too far. Beyond the un-reachable rifle jutting from the saddle boot, he saw South, Lind and Lodge coming along the street: fast and with guns drawn.

'It's what you wanted, kid!' he called, returning his attention to Mason.

Mason did not allow himself to be riled by the taunting word. His eyes and the rifle remained rock steady. 'And I'll get what I want, dude!' he answered.

'What's the idea?' Joe South demanded as he and his deputies lumbered to a panting, sweating halt.

The lawmen's guns hovered between the unmoving forms of Steele on the ground and Mason at the window of the doctor's house.

'But the Tyler bunch will make you pay harder than I ever could!' Mason yelled. And a tight smile curled up the corners of his mouth and showed a thin sliver of his teeth. His eyes remained like shiny pieces of pebble as they continued their fixed stare at the Virginian. 'What d'you think, sheriff? He blasted their man. Maybe they'll stay outta Black Rock if we hand him over to them.'

Behind the protection of the lawmen's guns, the crowd had deserted the body-laden stage to advance along the street.

'It's an idea, Joe,' Andy Lodge said. His eyes were as hard as Mason's as he glanced at Steele.

'Worth a try,' Curtis Lind added. And he even smiled.

South expressed deep concern. 'I don't like it,' he muttered.

'I'm with you, feller,' Steele rasped. He sat up slowly, aware that the rifle muzzle moved to remain aimed at his head.

The grey eyes in the burnished face of the sheriff were abruptly as cruel as the muzzles of the Colts he swung to aim at the Virginian. But the expression was just a façade.

88

A great deal of doubt lurked beneath the surface. 'I don't like it,' he repeated. 'But anythin's worth a try. Get up, mister!'

'You just lost me, feller,' the Virginian responded as he eased upright, wincing at the pain from his bruised shoulder.

'It's what we aim to do!' Lodge growled with a grin.

'He won't be no loss!' the familiar voice of Kate Porter taunted.

She was rewarded with a mumbling of assent from the crowd.

'Desperate situations call for desperate measures, Steele,' South said dully. Beads of salty moisture oozed out of his forehead and coursed down to drip off his eyelids. But with both Colts aimed at Steele, he could not wipe away the sweat.

'That's about the size of it,' the Virginian allowed evenly. A cold smile altered his mouthline. 'While you're the ruler around here '

CHAPTER SEVEN

As the Tyler gang rode out of the timber, a white flag was raised at the highest point in Black Rock. This was at the top of the church steeple. It could be clearly seen, for a cool evening breeze had breathed in from the east as the western dome of the sky reddened in announcement of the sunset to come.

It could also be clearly seen that the flag was one of truce rather than surrender. For, part way down Ogden Street, where the widely-spaced houses ended and the tightly packed business section began, a strong defensive line had been erected. The main structure, which stretched solidly from one sidewalk to the other, was comprised of the stage – still blood-stained but emptied of its corpses – and two buckboards tipped onto their sides. The gaps between and beneath were filled with bulging sacks and wired bales of hay, Men with guns at the ready stood behind the barricade, only their heads and shoulders visible to the approaching gang.

Although Olney Tyler and his men could not see it, a similar barricade had been erected at the end of Black Rock's other main street. They could see defenders on building roofs, positioned to meet an attack against either flank of the town. Some were men and some were women. The claim that the people of Black Rock would back the actions of their lawman was proved not to have been an idle boast.

Steele had been aware of this for the first few minutes he

spent in the sun-heated cell at the rear of the law office. For he had been able to hear the shouted instructions from South, then the noises of hectic activity as the town's citizens hurried to erect the barricades. He slept after that, in the certain knowledge there was no way out of the spartan cell unless with help from beyond the bars and solid concrete. He did not wake when a midday meal was slid under the door: and Curtis Lind, who delivered the food, did not attempt to rouse him.

When Lind returned, along with Lodge, the food was cold and spoiled by the broiling heat of the long afternoon. There was no opportunity to eat it, anyway.

'Guess who's comin' to get you, Steele,' Lodge rasped.

'Looks like the east and west of South,' Steele replied as he unfolded himself from the cot while Lind unlocked and swung open the barred door.

Both deputies had their Colts in the holsters. But each held a Winchester. They used the rifles to beckon him through the doorway. The sun was still bright through the building's windows and it wasn't until he stepped out on to the sidewalk that he felt the chillness of the early evening breeze. He looked towards the spot where his horse had been shot from under him. The mare, with his sheepskin coat and the rest of his gear, had been removed. Even the bloodstained dust had been blown away.

Lodge and Lind kept just the right distance behind him as the Virginian led the way along the street. The defenders up on the roofs and at the barricade divided their tense attention between his measured progress and the nine riders who had slowed their horses out on the trail. Not until he reached the barricade did Steele see a smiling face. Jack Mason, with a foot bandaged and an arm in a sling, leaned on a walking stick and grinned at the Virginian with evil triumph.

'Give my best to Pa, dude,' he rasped.

'He doesn't deserve anything as bad as your best, kid,' Steele answered.

Anger darkened Mason's ashen face. But he made only a twitchy move to draw. He had to let go of the stick, and he fell against a hay bale.

'You're winnin'!' South snarled at Mason. 'Be satisfied, kid.'

'Not just winnin', sheriff!' Mason responded, and worked the grin of triumph back on to his face. 'I've won.'

Hoofbeats at the gallop sounded from the other side of the barricade.

'Two of 'em comin' fast, Joe!' Hatcher reported from his vantage point looking across the roof of the stage. 'Rest held back.'

He gave Steele a look of pity, then, returned to his surveillance. The hoofbeats slowed and stopped.

'You people got somethin' you want to say before the shootin' starts?' a man with a deep voice called.

Like his deputies, South had armed himself with a Winchester. He levelled it at Steele and gave a curt nod. Lodge and Lind responded by moving forward and removing two heavy sacks from between the stage and an overturned buckboard.

'First shootin's at you, Steele. If you don't move on out.' South sounded tough. But the guilt in his face could have defused his intent. Except that the levelled Winchester cancelled this out.

'You're still being overpaid, feller,' Steele told him, and stepped into the opening.

The Virginian had not seen the two riders before. One of them was a Mexican, but he was not the Raul who had been in Black Rock earlier. This man was slimly built with a narrow moustache decorating a smooth-skinned face sculptured to a neat pattern of Latin good looks. He was in his early twenties. The other man was twice this age. A head taller at an inch or so above six feet, he had a bulky frame topped by a large head with a craggy face. Both had nervously suspicious dark eyes. And each held a rifle in a one-handed grip, with the stock resting on his thigh. Their skin was grimed deep with the dust of hot travel. Their ill-worn clothing was of a sombre hue.

As Steele stepped into view, each brought his other hand across to grip the rifle, ready to take aim.

'What is this?' the Mexican demanded to know.

'It's not a what,' South growled. 'It's a who. The guy who blasted your buddy.'

Both men leaned forward to stare hard at Steele. They expressed hatred, then anger, then puzzlement. The Mexican straightened first, and nodded.

'But if we kill him now, you kill us, I think, *senor* sheriff?'

'Get Tyler up here!' South ordered.

'Law boy's givin' us orders, Pedro,' the second man drawled. 'I don't like that.'

Pedro shrugged. 'Sometimes an *ombre* must do what he does not like to get what he likes.' He turned in his saddle and raised his Winchester to beckon with it. 'Olney!' he yelled. 'The sheriff, he wants to make deal.'

A man broke from the group of seven horsemen who waited two hundred yards off down trail. He held his mount to an easy canter and Pedro and the American moved to each side to allow the newcomer to stop between them.

Olney Tyler was as dirty and dishevelled as they were. A great deal older than both of them, he looked to be pushing sixty and was perhaps past the three score years. But there was nothing decrepit about him. He was tall and he was broad and not an ounce of his frame was excess fat. Beneath an ankle-length grey coat which was unbuttoned, he wore tight-fitting pants and shirt which mounded his muscular flesh. He had a round face, thickly and darkly stubbled. It would have been handsome had it not been for the cruel twist to his mouth and the harshness of his stare. This combination gave him an expression which made him look deranged. He carried a double-barrelled shotgun hung on his saddlehorn by a strap. Bandoliers criss-crossed his massive chest, slotted with cartridges.

'This is the *ombre* who wipe out Pete,' Pedro reported after the harsh eyes of Tyler had surveyed the barricade, Steele, and South who stood behind the Virginian.

'He's bounty huntin' for the whole lot of you!' Jack Mason called from behind the barricade.

Tyler slanted a cheroot into the corner of his mouth, but he did not light it. His hard eyes held on a position midway between the heads of Steele and South.

'Pete was a good man,' he said through teeth clenched around the cheroot. 'All my men are good men. I hate to lose any one of them.'

He took the cheroot from his mouth. But his teeth trapped the end and he chewed on the smoking tobacco.

'You can have him, Tyler,' South offered. 'Take him and do what you have to do. But don't come back to Black Rock after you're done.'

Tyler spat out the mess from his mouth and clamped his teeth around the shortened cheroot. 'What if I say no?'

'You get blasted where you sit, mister!' South snarled. 'Them two with you, likewise. A six-strong Tyler bunch without Tyler headin' them up – I figure we can take care of them. If they came back.'

The big bank robber had bitten off some more tobacco and chewed it. Now he spat it out.

'Sounds right,' he allowed. 'There's lots of banks in lots of other towns. But there's only one Olney Tyler.' He nodded. 'We'll take him!'

It was as if Joe South was afraid of time to have second

thoughts. He thrust out with the Winchester. The jab of the muzzle into Steele's back was both forceful and painful. With a grunt, he was shoved forward. As the Virginian took a short series of stumbling steps, Tyler jerked his horse sideways on. Steele crashed into the hindquarters of the animal. Tyler was old and he was big. But he was still fast. As Steele found his balance and stood erect, he looked up into the twin muzzles of the shotgun. It was aimed at the centre of his face from a range of six inches.

'You got anythin' to say for yourself, bastard?' the mounted man asked evenly.

'Go on, dude!' Jack Mason yelled. 'I wanna hear you beg for your life.'

'You want to, bastard?' Tyler asked.

'Don't want to lose my head, feller,' Steele said at a conversational level. Then he lowered his voice so that only Tyler and his two men could hear the words. 'But if I do, you lose a million dollars.'

Pedro expressed interest. The expressions of the other two did not alter by a degree.

'Not here, Tyler!' South yelled. 'Take him someplace and do it. The folks here have seen enough blood for one day.'

'I wanna see Steele's!' Mason countered, his demand high-pitched with anger.

'Get up behind Pedro, bastard!' The big man spat out some more tobacco. 'Any tricks and the nice people of Black Rock get to see a lot more blood.'

'Hey, Olney!' Pedro complained. 'That scattergun will kill me, too.'

'Sure enough will,' Tyler agreed. 'So you better see he don't pull nothin'.' Even when he grinned, he continued to express cruelty. 'See, bastard, it's other people blastin' my boys I don't go for. If I do it. . . .' He shrugged. 'Life can't be roses all the way, can it?'

'Sometimes there have to be lilies,' the Virginian responded as Pedro drew a foot from a stirrup to allow his passenger to mount the horse.

At the same time, South stepped back and the hole in the defences was plugged with the bags.

'Joe?' a man said loudly from behind the barricade. 'How we know they won't finish Steele and then come back here again?'

'We don't,' South acknowledged dully as all three horses were wheeled and commanded to the gallop.

The Virginian held on to Pedro's waist and knew he was as much a prisoner now as he had been in the cell. Pedro had a Remington in his tied-down holster and his Winchester was within easy reach in the boot. But Tyler, with the now quarter-size cheroot back between his teeth, rode level and ten feet to the side of the double-mounted horse. He held the reins with one hand while the other was fisted on the shotgun frame, finger curled around both triggers, and stock jammed against his hip.

The other six men of the gang were on the move, riding down the trail towards town, rifles at the ready to give covering fire. But no shots sounded from Black Rock. When the two groups met, the larger force swung their horses around to fall in behind Tyler, who shrugged off his guard duty to ride at point.

But, surrounded by a bunch of cold-blooded killers astride mounts who pounded the sun-baked hardness of the ground with shod hooves, Steele acknowledged that he was still the complete captive. He tasted fear on his tongue and the roof of his mouth and did not attempt to fool himself that it was dust that soaked up the moisture and left him parched. At any time of intense danger, fear was a healthy sensation. Another lesson of the terrible war that had helped him survive the violent peace.

Controlled fear heightend a man's awareness and kept him physically poised to follow the dictates of an alert consciousness. He had experienced it earlier, as he stepped out through the gap in the barricade. But not to the extent that he did now. While Tyler and his two men had been within easy shooting range of the town's firepower, there had been a chance Joe South would attempt to expunge his guilt.

So Steele had been afraid of the results of a burst of gunfire, and tensed to react in an attempt to survive. The odds had been long, but the chance had been there. It had slipped away. Now the odds were so long the chance was out of sight. But Steele stoked his fear, feeling the tension build in his brain and the tenseness flowing into his muscles. The chill air of the slipstream kept the sweat off his face. But he could smell himself as his odour became as gamey as that of the Mexican he rode with.

The trail took a final curve across the open terrain and then there was a hundred yard straight before the tight-knit group of riders plunged into the timber.

Like a cavalry officer at the end of a training charge, Olney Tyler held up an arm with his shotgun clutched in a fist. He slowed his horse and the others reined their mounts to match the slackening pace.

They came to a halt.

Pedro raised himself in the stirrups, as if to stretch. Instead, he bent suddenly at the waist. His rump smashed into Steele's belly and the Virginian was sent sliding over the horse's hindquarters. He flailed his legs, trying to land on his feet. But he hit the ground unbalanced and toppled. As he scrambled to his feet, Tyler and his men moved their horses into a circle. Steele made a slow turn and saw that he was covered by the shotgun, five Winchesters, two Spencers and an old Henry repeater.

'Say the word, Olney!' the gaunt-faced man invited. 'This is sure as hell the one who wiped out Pete. Me and Raul saw it.'

97

'*Si*,' the second Mexican in the bunch confirmed.

The rest of the men were all of European stock. Many shapes and sizes and ages. The common denominator among them was that each looked like the cold-blooded killer he was. Steele knew that indefinable look for, when the circumstances were appropriate, he wore it himself. Sheriff Mason of Crest City had not been the first man to note it. And he knew that Joe South back in Black Rock had perceived it – but without mentioning it or attempting to capitalise on it, as the Crest City lawman had.

'How about three words?' Tyler offered. 'One million dollars.'

'Words are cheap, *senor*,' Pedro growled. 'I heard that, too.'

'But his life ain't cheap.' This from the other man who had gone to the barricade. 'He comes high if he can deliver.'

'Where's the loot, bastard?' Tyler wanted to know, chewing and spitting out the final mess of tobacco from the cheroot.

Steele ignored the others, knowing that Tyler was the only man he had to convince. 'The vault in the Black Rock Bank,' he replied.

The grin was suddenly back on the cruel face. But only for a moment. Tyler looked hard down into Steele's un-afraid face.

'Lousy try, bastard.' This was from the man with the deep set eyes and sunken cheeks.

'Hold it, Gus!' Tyler growled, still thoughtful. 'This guy ain't no tinhorn just in from Boston.'

'What you mean, *senor*?' the fat Mexican said.

The thin one spat. 'He's no smart *ombre*, either, Olney. He let himself get caught by those three lawmen jokers.'

'Some bad luck from out of right field,' Steele excused.

Tyler continued to study the Virginian as the impatience of his men mounted.

'Let's blast him and get back to town, Olney,' a youngster of about eighteen urged. 'There ain't no million bucks in the bank.'

'And even if there is, we don't need this bastard to get it.'

Tyler hooked his shotgun strap over his saddlehorn and took out another cheroot. 'He's bettin' his life we do need him,' the gang leader mused, and bit off a wad of tobacco. He chewed with obvious enjoyment of the taste. 'And since he ain't no tinhorn just in from Boston, I figure he could have somethin'.'

'But Olney, he wiped out Pete,' somebody complained.

Tyler spat out chewed tobacco and interrupted his appraisal of Steele to rake his harsh eyes around the circle of mounted men. His glower was sufficient to silence the arguments forming on the lips of others. 'Just sit and listen, you guys. We ain't got nothin' to lose but time. And them folks back there ain't about to lift up the damn bank and carry it off into hidin'.' His gaze returned to Steele. 'Okay, bastard,' he invited. 'Tell us why we need you?'

'What's your plan for the raid?'

Tyler spat out a length of cheroot as soon as he bit it off. 'You ain't here to ask no questions, bastard!'

'I didn't even know he was here to answer them,' a man rasped.

'You made a deal with South and his deputies, right?'

'Damn lawman talked!'

'Not to this bastard,' Tyler countered the assumption.

The Virginian launched into a fast explanation while Tyler was still intrigued. 'You were wound up to take the bank last night. Not when you hit town, but after you spread around some of the Crest City money on booze and then found out there were no women for you.'

'We weren't happy, that's for sure,' a man muttered.

'Let the bastard talk, Ray,' Tyler growled.

'And in that kind of mood, you weren't about to take orders from three small town lawmen,' Steele went on. 'Unless there was a good reason.'

Tyler waved the remains of his cheroot around the circle of men. 'You don't look it on the outside, bastard,' he said. 'But down in your guts you're shit scared. These men and their guns are the reason. South and his boys got the drop on us.'

The Virginian raised a wry smile. 'Heavy odds against me. Last night you were the nine to three favourites, feller. And you're not like South, Tyler. You just don't talk about taking risks. You take them. But last night you and your men rode out of Black Rock like you were on a Sunday School outing. And today...'

He looked to his left and right and, in the falling darkness of night among the timber, he had difficulty in recognising faces. But he spotted the gaunt-faced Gus and the fat Mexican, Raul '... this feller and that one ... he pointed to the men, '... and Salter rode back in again. In broad daylight, with the sheriff and deputies looking on, they checked over the bank.'

'He talks like he's a lawman himself, Olney,' Gus growled suspiciously.

Tyler shook his head, still deeply intrigued by Steele. 'Lawmen are dumb. They gotta be to do their kinda job for their kinda money. This is one smart bastard.'

He made to take another bite from the cheroot, then looked at it with distaste and crushed it in the palm of his hand. He hurled the mess of tobacco away and then hooked his thumb to jerk it this time towards Raul.

'Get mounted again, bastard,' he ordered. 'And stay smart. You don't, and you and the Mex will ride outta this world into the next.'

'Olney, why is it always me who must be at risk?' Raul asked in a whining tone.

'Don't you like the rest of us?' Tyler asked him with mocking hurt. 'You want Gus or Pedro, or Ray or maybe me to be in the firin' line?'

The others grinned. Raul grimaced and booted his Spencer with low keyed anger. Then he kicked free of a stirrup and glowered an ill-tempered invitation for Steele to mount behind him. 'If you get me killed, *senor*,' he rasped as the Virginian swung up across the horse, 'I promise you that my ghost will haunt your ghost.'

Tyler spoke in low tones to the two men flanking him. These broke from the circle and closed in on the horse carrying Raul and Steele. Like the others, these men had booted their rifles. But each drew a Navy Colt as they assumed their role as guards.

'You ain't the only smart one around here, bastard!' Tyler said with heavy menace. 'You ain't the only guy can find out a couple of details and fill in the rest for himself. You been talkin' and I been thinkin'. You're sayin' South and his sidekicks are fixin' to double-cross me. Right, bastard?'

Steele shrugged. 'If South didn't come close to a million, it seems he reckons to outsmart you, feller.'

Tyler spat. Plain saliva without the pulp of tobacco. But the globule of moisture hit a tree trunk with a forceful sound. 'Fifteen grand ain't at all close to a million, bastard!'

'A long way off, I reckon,' Steele answered evenly.

'Just like you're a long way off of gettin' turned loose, bastard,' the cruel-faced man countered as the gang jostled their horses into a riding formation, with Tyler in the lead.

The Virginian glanced at his two guards with their drawn Colts and then surveyed the surrounding timber. 'I'm sure enough not out the wood yet,' he acknowledged softly.

CHAPTER EIGHT

THE money drop was on the eastern shore of the lake, hidden from town by a narrow inlet of water that cut between high timber. A pathway of trodden brush indicated it was a spot well used by the citizens of Black Rock. The way through the brush was only wide enough to allow the gang to pass in single file. The reluctant Raul was instructed to take the lead. Tyler rode in the number two position of the line, with his cocked shotgun aimed over his mount's head at Steele's back. Just enough moonlight filtered through the overhead foliage for each man to see the one in front of him.

Then, abruptly, the track opened out into a clearing with close-growing trees and dense brush on three sides and the head of the inlet on the other. A large rock humped from the moon-silvered surface of the inlet and Steele saw how the town had received its name. The rock was a shiny black.

'This is a bad place, Olney,' Raul whispered apprehensively as the men moved their horses onto the springy turf of the clearing.

The others showed they shared his feelings by drawing handguns or unbooting their rifles.

'This ain't our way, Olney,' Gus rasped.

Steele dismounted before the Mexican had an opportunity to shove him off. But he kept his actions slow and smooth, aware that Tyler had made only a fast survey of his surroundings and refixed his concentration on his prisoner.

'What we got to lose except a few lives?' Tyler growled. 'The two Mexes, Ray and Jervis! Into the trees and cover us.'

All the men dismounted and those named split into two pairs and beat at the brush with their rifle stocks to force their way into cover. A short, bald-headed man was put in charge of the horses, which he led into a corner of the clearing. Then Tyler motioned with the shotgun for Steele to move across to the lake's edge, where the wind-ruffled water was lapping half-heartedly at the reedy bank.

Tyler stood behind him. Gus took up a position on one side and the two remaining members of the gang stepped up on the other side.

An owl hooted off in the dense timber. All other wild life was silent, biding its time before accepting the intrusion of the men. Then Gus spoke.

'Shouldn't we oughta look around, Olney? Maybe one of them law boys was here already and left the bundle.'

'I told 'em to wait,' Tyler rasped, his tone of voice suggesting he had another cheroot between his teeth. 'You know that. You was there and heard.'

'Yeah, but what with the trouble and all – maybe they got scared.'

'They been scared all along,' Tyler rasped. 'We wait!'

The Virginian looked down into the reeds and out along the inlet to where it broadened into the lake. It was obvious someone was scheduled to come to the clearing by water. He reflected that it would be a wry coincidence if he ended up in the reedy water with a bullet in his head. The way Hank Jaggs had done to start the chain of events which brought him here.

'Why did Salter and the other two go in to check the bank?' Steele asked after stretched seconds of silence.

Tyler spat out some chewed tobacco. Then he laughed, and it was an odd sound from such a large, brutal man. It was the same laughter Steele had heard in the canyon after the massacre of the posse. Very high-pitched, to the point that it had a girlish quality.

'So you don't know everythin', bastard?' he taunted.

Steele shrugged. 'No one knows everything, feller. If I was that smart, I wouldn't be here.'

'You're close to a lot of bounty money, bastard.'

Steele glanced over his shoulder and showed a thin smile. 'Let me know when you're ready to surrender, feller.'

Tyler vented his feminine laughter again, and it sounded even odder now that Steele was looking at him. For his face was incapable of displaying the kind of mirth that sounded from his throat. 'So you got suckered, bastard. Pete, Gus and Raul went into Black Rock to check we weren't being suckered. I wanted the bank cased to take account of South not delivering.'

'And if South had arrested them?'

Tyler bit, chewed and spat. 'We lost one man, bastard. And I guess you saw the way we didn't let that ride. South's deal was the money and no killin'. But you screwed him up on that, didn't you, bastard? But it only changed the deal a little. The money and no more killin'.'

'He's comin', Olney!' Gus whispered, levelling his rifle out along the inlet and pumping the action.

There was just one man in a rowboat. He was not an expert oarsman, or perhaps it was just that he was nervous. The blades splashed water and the bow of the tiny craft zigzagged as he steered around the hump of the black rock. He kept looking over his shoulder, as much to peer at the waiting men as to check his course.

'That you, Tyler?' he called when he was still ten yards from shore.

He had been nothing but a dark silhouette against the water until he spoke. The voice named him as Joe South.

'I sure ain't St Peter!' Tyler yelled in reply. 'But could be you'll get to meet him soon.'

The Black Rock sheriff gave the boat a final thrust, then shipped his oars to allow it to coast into the shore. Nobody moved to help him and he had to step over the side into the shallow water as the bows snagged among the reeds. He dragged the boat in closer, until it was firmly lodged in the mud, then reached back into it and lifted out a sack.

'Doesn't look a million dollars heavy,' Steele said softly.

The tall, broad frame of South froze for a moment. Then he straightened and turned, the sack swinging from a hand that trembled. He stared in fear and confusion at Steele, switched his attention to Tyler, then back to Steele.

'What is this?' he demanded.

'Not a this,' Steele replied, paraphrasing the lawman's own words of earlier. 'A who.'

Gus stepped forward and snatched the sack from South's hand. The sheriff made no attempt to stop him. Now he had both hands free. For a part of a second he looked sorely tempted to use them in going for his guns. He went instead for words.

'I should have blasted you on Ogden Street, Steele!' he spat out. Then he swung his hard eyes towards Tyler. Anger had replaced his initial fear. 'We made a deal.' He pointed to the sack which Gus had opened. 'And there's my part, in spite of what happened to the stage.'

Tyler prodded the shotgun forward to nudge Steele gently in the back. 'This here bastard reckons we made a lousy deal, mister lawman. Says as how there's a million in the vault.'

South's lips gaped in a silent gasp. He stared hard into Steele's face, but the impassively set features were totally unresponsive. 'That's ... that's plain crazy!' he spluttered.

'He's tryin' to save his neck is all. Why the hell would a bank in a town like Black Rock have a million dollars in its vault?'

'I wondered about that,' Tyler admitted, and it was obviously not a spur-of-the-moment comment. He had considered the point.

'And even if it did,' South went on hurriedly, with a background tone of triumph. 'How the hell would a drifter like Steele know about it?'

'Wondered about that as well,' Tyler allowed. The shotgun nudged the back of the Virginian again. 'You wanna tell about that, bastard? On account that if it don't make no sense, we can dump off our extra baggage right here.'

Gus had been delving his hands into the sack, bringing out fistfuls of bills and thrusting them back inside again. 'Looks to be about the fifteen grand the law boy said it would be, Olney,' he reported.

'Fifteen and a couple of hundred over the top,' South said quickly. 'I cleaned out . . .'

Both barrels of the shotgun exploded. The sound was deafening within the confines of the clearing. Steele felt the draught of the slipstream as the charges were forced through the air. The blast rocked him to the side. The muzzle flashes blinded him for a moment. And then his vision cleared while his ears were still singing and popping with the effects of the noise.

South's square-shaped head with its chiselled features was blasted off his shoulders. Only the hat, still firmly fixed in place, showed it had once been a human head. As it sailed through the air in a graceful arc it looked like an overripe melon that had been skinned and hit with a sledgehammer. The crimson juice and chunks of pulpy flesh dropped from it as its arc decayed. Then it plopped into the lake water. Night shrouded the smoke-like red trails it left as it sank to the bottom.

The decapitated body stood erect for a part of a second, with blood spouting up in a torrent from the meaty wound. Then it toppled backwards, dying nerves causing the arms and legs to twitch. It fell into the rowboat and the weight and impact of the body shoved the bows out of the mud. The boat floated slowly away from the shore, as if in search of the sunken head to make Joe South whole again.

The shock of the brutal killing left Steele as unmoved as Tyler and the other men in the clearing. And his own lack of emotion did not surprise him. Death was not his business. He had no business. But death in many forms was seldom far away. He lived with it and had long ago used up his reserves of human emotions. He did not even feel resentment that Tyler had got to Joe South first. South had been doomed to die when he handed over his prisoner to Tyler. The individual behind the killing gun did not matter.

When the Virginian turned to look at Tyler, he saw the tall man was ejecting the still-smoking cartridges from the shotgun. But other guns were covering Steele.

'He served his purpose,' Tyler said dully and slotted two fresh cartridges into the breeches of the shotgun.

'Blast him and let's get out, Olney,' Ray called from in the trees. 'Fifteen grand for no sweat ain't bad. And South was right about this guy, I figure. Just shootin' off his mouth to keep from gettin' his head shot off.'

Tyler listened patiently, then snapped the gun closed and angled it up at Steele's head. He eased back the hammers. 'Well, bastard?'

Tension, sprung from the source of fear, flowed to every muscle in the Virginian's body. It had been a gamble ever since he surrendered to South and the deputies as he lay beside his dead horse on Ogden Street. But now he was running out of cards to play: and without cards a man could not even rely on luck.

'The million came in on the morning train. You had one man dead and the other two running when it was put into the bank vaults.'

Steele's voice was as calm as his expression. Inside, his nerve ends tingled and his muscles were so taut they ached. This was the last chapter in a piecemeal story he had been composing from the moment he mentioned the one million dollar bait to Tyler. At the barricade; on the trail through the timber; and here as Joe South rowed the boat up the inlet, for there had always been a chance the lawman was using him as more than a human sacrifice. Instead, a human plaything for Tyler to toy with while a surprise attack was mounted and launched.

But South had never been anything but what he seemed. His deal with the Tyler bunch had been on the level. And not because he was a coward. He would not have brought the money to the drop himself if he had been that. He had simply been a small town sheriff endeavouring to protect the citizens of that town from a gang of wanton killers. And, because a stranger had been the catalyst of sudden and violent death in that town, he had experienced only a mild degree of guilt in sacrificing that stranger. The Virginian knew he had only to admit he was lying. The barrels of the shotgun would again belch violent death and the Tyler bunch would ride on. Joe South would not have died in vain.

But Steele owed South nothing. He owed Joe South's town nothing. It was the other way around. They had pushed him to the brink of death and life was all he possessed. So they owed him. He could not repay the sheriff, whose headless corpse was still floating gently down the inlet. But the town was virtually untouched by the violence of either himself or the Tyler bunch.

'In a big crate with a label that said one million dollars, eh, bastard?' Tyler taunted.

108

'In railroad company express crates,' Steele replied evenly. 'And I knew what was in them because I've been planning to get them for two months.'

'A two-bit bounty hunter?' one of the men in the trees yelled.

'Ambition doesn't buy any beef and beans,' the Virginian pointed out, talking directly to Tyler who was again showing intrigued interest. 'A feller has to eat while he plans.'

He knew he had only one other marked card left in his hand. On its value – the value placed upon it by Tyler – rested his sole chance of survival. And he had to play it fast. The big man in the long coat was sold on the million dollar lie. So Steele was relegated to the same position as Joe South after the lawman had delivered the goods. He had served his purpose.

Tyler's finger tightened around the two triggers of the shotgun.

'We don't need him to check it out, Olney,' Gus said.

Steele tensed himself, without making a visible move, to go for the water. As a last resort means of escape.

'Fifty-fifty split, feller,' he said resisting the impulse to hurl out the words fast. 'And I'll get you into the bank and out. Without a drop of sweat, let alone blood.'

The trigger finger relaxed without uncurling. The girlish laughter was just a short burst. 'Spillin' blood is part of my business, bastard. I got more bullet wounds than you got holes to sweat through.'

'But no one lives forever.'

'You not live at all from now, *senor*, I think!' Raul called from his hiding place.

Tyler's grin accentuated the cruel twist of his mouthline. 'Hey, Mex!' he yelled. And he lowered the shotgun, switching its aim from Steele's head to his belly. 'Mount up, but leave room for a passenger.' He raked his eyes around the clearing. 'All of you, mount up!'

'Me again!' Raul groaned.

'You mean you're buyin' his story, Olney?' the bald-headed man in charge of the horses asked incredulously.

'Not for no fifty per cent of the take I ain't,' Tyler growled. 'But I got what it takes to hammer out better terms than that.'

He slapped the shotgun barrels against the palm of his hand.

'I'm always ready to talk a deal,' the Virginian responded.

Tyler nodded. 'You been doin' good at that so far, bastard.'

'But you'd just better be able to deliver more than talk, mister!' Gus warned. 'Better like one million dollars cash.'

Steele glanced down the inlet as the men headed for their horses. The rowboat had floated around the black rock and was beginning to pitch and yaw gently as it was caught by the less calm surface of the breeze-rippled lake.

'One million,' he promised, and shuddered as the chill night wind found a way under his jacket and cut through his vest and shirt to raise goose bumps on his flesh.

'That is a big amount for such a small man, *senor*,' Raul rasped. 'Even to think about.'

'I've been thinking about it a lot lately,' Steele replied as a stirrup was left empty for him again. 'While I've still got a head for figures.'

CHAPTER NINE

THE clock above the impressive entrance of the Black Rock Ranchers and Farmers Association Building struck the hour of two. The strident clangs awoke Kate Porter and John Hatcher. As the town's most senior citizens, it was to be expected that they would feel the effects of so many hours of watching and waiting. They accepted this privilege due to their years, and experienced no guilt for their lack of attention. Hatcher resumed his surveillance from behind the stage as if sleep had never interrupted it. The elderly woman strained her eyes to peer out over the lake from the roof of her boarding house.

Both were covered by younger people charged with watching the same areas from similar vantage points.

The regular chiming of the clock had been the only loud noises to sound within the town's barricades since they had been erected. The explosion of the shotgun's discharge had come from outside the barricades – deep in the timber at the lake shore. And the response it had drawn from the citizens of Black Rock had been low-keyed.

Joe South was dead. Everyone knew that and everyone had known it was the likely result when they watched him row the tiny boat across the lake towards Black Rock Creek. So there had been some sad-eyed glances exchanged, a few tears shed and countless prayers said for his soul – silently and aloud.

After that, it was just a matter of waiting and watching.

111

For the sheriff had been unable to offer any guarantees – whichever way the trip to the creek ended for him.

Now, four hours of bitterly cold night had passed since the shotgun had blasted the distant silence for a split-second. And it was over three hours since the rowboat had drifted into view, only to be swept by a current into the deep shadows of a timber shrouded bank. The Tyler gang had made no move against the town and the more optimistic of its citizens were beginning to lose the edge off their alertness. Tyler and his men had slaughtered eight people on the stage and now Joe South. The gang also had every cent out of the bank vault. With each cold minute that was chipped from the present and stacked into the past, it seemed more and more likely the outlaws were satisfied they had avenged the life of the man they had lost.

But many others were not so confident. And Jack Mason, hobbling on his injured foot with the aid of the walking stick, did everything in his power to stoke these doubts. Andy Lodge and Curtis Lind played their parts in this, too. A shotgun blast had signalled the death of Sheriff Joe South. But nothing had been heard or seen to prove that Adam Steele had been killed. And the Virginian had as good a reason to hold a grudge against Black Rock as the Tyler gang.

And a man like Steele . . .

Always the encouragement to stay awake and alert finished with this hanging sentence. And then there were the final words of Joe South to recall:

'Don't you folks take nothin' for granted, you hear,' he had told the crowd gathered in front of the bank on Ogden Street. 'There never was no guarantee, 'cause men like the Tyler bunch can't never be relied on to keep their word. But when I saw that bunch ride into our town, I figured it was worth a try. So I made the deal. Everythin' in the bank and no raid or shootin'. Mr Harvey of the bank backed me and I'm hopin' you will. A man's life is worth all the money in the world. And wouldn't have been no lives lost if it hadn't been for the bounty huntin' stranger who started trouble.'

His gaze had swept over the faces of his audience then, and become fixed for a moment on Jack Mason. Long enough for the injured youngster to be made aware the lawman held him partially responsible for the killings. But not so long as to attract the attention of the crowd to Mason.

'Could be there'll be another killin' out where I'm supposed to meet up with Tyler and his men. But you folks pay me to take risks and this is one I'm prepared to take. But don't you take no risks you don't have to, you hear. You keep the barricades up and you keep watchin' until sun up.'

There had been some argument – not against the plan to surrender the money: but against Joe South going out alone to meet the Tyler bunch. He silenced it with the unassailable counter that to risk more lives would defeat the object of the deal.

So he went out through the barricade and the people of Black Rock waited and watched. Then came the gunshot and the drifting rowboat. First came grief for Joe South. Then anger at the Tyler bunch for killing him – even hope in some hearts that the gang would ride in so they could be made to pay for their crime. But, as inaction caused time to drag and the night's cold grew more bitter the watchers at the barricades and on the rooftops began to feel gratitude. Gratitude towards their sheriff for giving his life so that they and their town remained secure from attack. And then they grew weary of a task that seemed increasingly futile with each silent minute that passed.

And Mason, Lodge and Lind had to move up and down

the streets between the barricades, warning the people to stay alert.

But despite the success of these warnings, Adam Steele was able to get the Tyler gang into Black Rock unobserved.

'You ain't just a smart talker, are you, bastard?' Olney Tyler growled as he joined the group at the railroad depot building and massaged his aching back.

He wasn't the only member of the gang with aching muscles. All of them were suffering the effects of crawling better than half a mile on their hands and knees. For it was that distance out along the railroad track to where a stand of cedars provided the closest patch of cover for the horses to the south of Black Rock.

And an approach from the south was important, as Steele had explained just before the men moved out into single file between the rails and dropped to the ties. Joe South had made his deal because he knew the people of Black Rock were inexperienced fighters. The Virginian had seen the town's defences for himself and all the action of the day had been to the north. The untrained defenders expected trouble – if it came – to spring from the north. But there were watchers on the rooftops, able to look across every line of advance if they chose. Which was why Steele suggested the Tyler bunch should crawl over the track ties: their dark forms merging with the cinders between the gleaming rails.

'This ain't our way, Olney!' the gaunt-faced Gus complained yet again.

The tall, skinny man had done a lot of whining on the long, circuitous ride from the lakeside timber to the stand of cedars on the other side of Black Rock. And he had the backing of most of the others, who were reluctant to switch from their usual method of riding openly on a bank: guns drawn – and blasting if anyone stood in their way.

But, at the cedars, a glowering Tyler had managed to silence all except the disgruntled Gus. The switch to the hostage ploy at Crest City had worked fine. And so had the deal with the sheriff of Black Rock.

'So why not move on out?' Gus had wanted to know. 'We scored good both places, Olney. And we only got the bastard's word that law boy shortchanged us here.'

'We got his word and we got him,' Tyler had countered, fixing Steele with his brutal grin. 'And if his word ain't worth nothin', his life sure as hell ain't.'

The eighteen-year-old Ray had led the crawling file of men. Tyler had brought up the rear, immediately behind Steele.

I'd say you was an officer in the war,' Tyler said when Steele failed to respond to his first comment at the railroad depot.

'Only a lieutenant,' the Virginian answered, moving to the corner of the building from where he could look along the lengths of the two main streets to the barricades at the far ends.

'He fought for the Rebels, I know,' the fat Raul supplied.

The short, bald-headed man spat. 'I hate working with losers,' he growled.

Tyler stuck a cheroot into his mouth. But he sucked it instead of biting off a length to chew. 'Losers try real hard to be winners,' he rasped, and levelled the shotgun at Steele's back. 'But luck can swing either way.'

The Virginian turned from making his surveillance and shivered. Not because he saw the twin muzzles of the shotgun pointing at him. Without the sheepskin coat, the cold seemed to be attacking him right down to his bone marrow. He eyed the tall man in the long coat quizzically.

'Like Gus keeps tellin' us, bastard,' Tyler said around

the cheroot. 'This ain't our way. But I can blast you now and make it our way.'

His men moved into a tight knit group behind him — safe from the scattering shot of the twin barrels should Tyler squeeze the two triggers.

'Your decision, feller,' Steele offered softly. The fear inside again poised him for a desperate, last resort escape bid.

'I don't like not havin' my horse, Olney,' the scar-faced man named Jervis put in nervously. 'And the bastard got us this far.'

'That's what I mean about luck,' Tyler answered. 'It's been good to the bastard so far. He's got us this close to the bank without even a scratch from a prickly pear. That's a lot of luck he's used up. His time could run out any friggin' second. And we don't know how he figures to get into that bank vault down the street.'

Steele showed a wry grin. 'A feller who counts on luck is just waiting for his number to come up, I reckon,' he said. He tapped his temple with a gloved finger. 'It's what's up here that's keeping me alive. Now, you coming my way or going yours?'

He turned his back on the men and stepped out into the open. He had to cross a gap of twenty feet from the corner of the depot building to the covered sidewalk in front of a hardware store. He could have been spotted by one of the watchers, or Tyler could have blasted a massive hole in his back. But no citizen of Black Rock was looking towards the depot. And the harsh eyes of Olney Tyler showed him there was no immediate escape the way Steele was going.

The sweat of fear oozing from Steele's pores immediately turned ice cold on his flesh. The twenty feet had looked like a mile. And when he gained the sidewalk and turned to look back, he felt as if it had been two miles and he had sprinted every inch.

116

There could be no talk across the gap, for voices would carry in the silent town. And Steele felt the tension drain out of him. If Tyler had intended to back his threat with action, he would have done it before now. A hiss of whispered words urged the men to follow in the Virginian's footsteps across the gap. While his men glowered, Tyler looked set to rasp another low-voiced warning at Steele. But the Virginian put a finger to his lips, turned, and moved on the balls of his feet along the sidewalk. He heard the tiny sounds of the men as they trailed him, But they were not the only noises in Black Rock. The town was by no means so silent as it had seemed when the fear of blasting death had been pounding in Steele's ears.

Some of the watchers were engaged in whispered conversations. Others shifted their feet and swung their arms to keep up the circulation against the cold. From the church came the cry of a baby whose sleep had been disturbed – revealing where the children and possibly the infirmed of Black Rock had been gathered.

Barring accidents, there was little chance of the intruders being spotted until they reached the corner of the cross street, for the buildings and their galleries kept the sidewalk in deep moon shadow. But there was a wide breach in the cover from the feed and seed store to Kate Porter's boarding house on the opposite corner.

'Okay, smart bastard?' Tyler rasped softly. 'What now?'

'Give me a rifle, feller,' Steele said evenly.

There was a sharp intake of breath. Every man vented the gasp, but it sounded like one noise alone. And it might have been the prelude to a series of curses. Except that each man realised where he was before he could explode his shock. The shotgun swung down to aim at Steele's belly from a range of no more than six inches.

'It ain't the time or place for jokes, bastard!' Tyler rasped.

Steele's cold-pinched face was impassive, concealing his frustration. It was important that the Tyler bunch as a whole or just one of their number betrayed their presence in town. If the signal came from him, he would be dead a moment later. If from the gang ... he had a chance. But they had all controlled their anger.

He turned just his head to look along the street. The guards behind the barricade were not in moon shadow. They could be clearly seen against the stage, the over-turned wagons, the bales and the sacks. He recognised Mason, Lind, Lodge, Hatcher and the bank clerk, Alvin Rhodes. There were three other men and four women he did not know by name or sight.

'This town's got no stomach for fighting, feller,' he whispered, returning his attention to Tyler. 'If he had to, South could have given it to them. Now there are just the two deputies and the kid from Crest City. With them dead, you've got it made.'

Tyler bit through his cheroot, and spat out the wad without chewing it. The anger held inside him coloured his face and glinted from his eyes. 'To keep a million bucks, they'll fight, bastard.'

Steele shook his head. 'Railroad money, feller?'

'I don't like it, Olney,' Ray rasped. 'Blast him and let's get.'

Tyler looked from Steele, to his men, and then at the citizens of Black Rock – up on the roofs and at the barricades. Finally, back at Steele. 'It's a lousy plan, bastard!' he accused.

Steele nodded towards Ray. 'I reckon it's better than his, feller.'

'I don't like it, either,' Jervis whispered, stroking his Winchester. 'It could be a trick.'

Tyler took the cheroot from his teeth without biting off any more, and dropped it to the sidewalk. 'Without the plan, we got nothin',' he growled. 'And if it's a trick, the bastard's as dumb as the law boy was. Not smart at all. Give him your rifle, Jervis.'

There was reluctance, but no argument. The Winchester was handed to Steele, barrel first. Jervis drew a revolver and it, like the shotgun and the other rifles, pointed menacingly at the Virginian.

As Steele took the Winchester, he felt a flicker of regret that it wasn't the Colt Hartford. Then the tension was back inside him. But it was a different brand now, as he dropped down on to one knee and eased the rifle stock against his shoulder. Fear was pushed into the background by a stronger sensation. That of hatred. An ice cold hatred that caused every muscle in his body to be as rock steady as those in his gloved trigger finger.

Four men had been responsible for driving him into the hands of the Tyler bunch. Joe South was already dead.

He waited until Jack Mason moved, turning to look back along Ogden Street and then taking a tentative step with the aid of the walking stick.

The Winchester cracked; and the wounded youngster was thrown back against the stage, the final pump action of his heart torrenting blood from the chest wound.

The boy's dying father had asked Steele to go easy on Jack. Steele had tried to. But a couple of flesh wounds had enabled the kid to make a second try for Steele.

The rifle swung as everyone at the barricade whirled to stare in horror at the toppling, bloody form of the boy. At the start of the violent peace, the Virginian had made the mistake of allowing his enemies to live too long. And, because of this error, he had been forced to kill his best friend.

Just as now, a second explosion from the Winchester killed Andy Lodge. The deputy took the shot in the side of his head. The bullet went right the way through and the

119

man's brains gushed out of his skull to stain the ground on which he fell.

Shouts of alarm and screams of horror counterpointed the third shot from the Winchester. Curtis Lind took the bullet in the throat as he tried to make a crouching run. He spun in a complete circle, spraying blood from a severed jugular vein. And, before he collapsed to the street, the answering fire cracked out of the night.

His hatred salved, Steele felt fear powering his escape bid. He lunged from his one-leg kneeling position into a humped-backed run. A hail of lead thudded into the street, the sidewalk and the building front. And the cursing men behind him scrambled for cover. Their guns exploded, but not towards him. The fear of death thrust them into firing at those who threatened them.

Two men screamed.

Steele rounded the corner of the store and threw himself full-length into the street. Bullets from the rooftops smacked into the ground around him. He forced himself into a roll – gaining the cover of the sidewalk planking.

Another man dropped onto the spot he had vacated. Prone and minus his gun. His hat was off and two holes in his hairless head oozed grey-flecked crimson. More bullets made dull sounds as they penetrated the unfeeling flesh of Baldy.

Steele felt drops of warm liquid splashing on to his face. It was blood from another man, spurting from his body and finding a way down through cracks in the sidewalk.

'Bastard! Bastard! Bastard!'

Tyler's voice shrieked through the barrage of gunfire and screams of anger and terror and agony. His shotgun roared twice in quick succession.

A man streaked across the street to the doorway of Kate Porter's boarding house. Steele powered himself out from under the sidewalk and raced in the wake of the man. Two figures toppled off the roof and thumped to the street on either side of the Virginian. Kate Porter and a man who waited on tables in her dining room. The force of shot from Tyler's gun had spilled dripping entrails from their bellies.

'The bastard called it wrong, I think,' Pedro rasped from the doorway as Steele leapt onto the sidewalk, bullets cracking around him. Then: 'Oh no – '

Steele was too close to use the rifle. He streaked a hand to his throat and caught hold of one weighted corner of his scarf. He let the rifle fall as the scarf came free of his neck and swung through the air. The thin Mexican went for his holstered revolver. Steele leaned towards him and flicked his wrist. The other weighted corner of the scarf curled around the Mexican's neck and Steele shot up his free hand under the wrist of the engaged one. He caught the second weight and crossed his forearms. The silk of the thuggee's scarf became taut around the filthy neck. Pedro dropped his revolver and tried to hook his fingers under the silk. But it was too tight.

Steele moved forward, pushing Pedro backwards. Bullets smashed into the doorframe. From the rooftops and from in front of the building on the opposite corner. Pedro went down on to his knees. His eyes bulged and his skin colour seemed to turn black. His tongue protruded and he went suddenly limp. As Steele slackened the scarf, the Mexican's dying breath smelled like a cesspit.

The Virginian whirled and snatched up the Winchester. A glance across the street showed him there were at least five of the Tyler gang still in the fight. Pedro was dead behind him. Baldy lay still in the street. The man who had dropped blood on to Steele was Jervis. The young Ray was sprawled half on the sidewalk and half into the street around the corner on the main street.

Gunfire was exploding from the doorway and windows

of the feed and seed store, but there was no way of knowing how many of the unseen five men were firing.

Steele turned and went further inside the boarding house. Then out of the rear door from the kitchen. The intervening buildings muted the gunfire a little as he moved stealthily towards the back lots of the block housing the law office.

He didn't think himself as smart as Tyler had kept telling him he was. Simply that Tyler and his men were dumb. They had failed to realise a simple fact – that, irrespective of whether there was a million dollars in the bank or not, the eruption of sudden death amongst them would spur the people of Black Rock to retaliate against the intruders. Without time to consider the consequences, reaction to sudden action was instinctive.

And the sight of other shattered bodies – Kate Porter, the waiter and perhaps more local citizens – stoked the instincts for revenge.

There was no rear door to the law office. Steele had to go down the alley at the side of the newspaper building. Then dash along the sidewalk and turn into the front entrance. But no shots were cracked towards him. The attention of the citizens of Black Rock was focused on the remnants of the Tyler bunch and vice versa.

He located his gear in an untidy heap in a corner of the office, behind Joe South's desk. The Colt Hartford was leaning against it. His actions slow and calm against the background of the gun battle, the Virginian discarded the Winchester and donned the sheepskin coat. Then he slotted the knife into his boot sheath and canted the Colt Hartford to his shoulder. His dark eyes were utterly cold as his mouthline formed into a grin of satisfaction. He felt whole again. A complete man. The complete killer: if that was the way it had to be. And a lot of the time, it had to be that way.

But not now. He had done his share of killing. And the people of Black Rock deserved to taste the sweetness of revenge. So he dropped into Joe South's chair and put his feet up on to the desk. The gunfire and the yells and screams went on.

'You didn't start the war you lost, feller,' he told himself. 'Maybe this time . . .'

CHAPTER TEN

THE first grey light of a cold dawn was streaking the eastern sky when the final shot of the battle of Black Rock was fired. Steele heard it from far off and knew which side had won. It had just been a matter of time and blood. Weight of numbers had made the bare result a foregone conclusion.

He waited in the cedars for a full fifteen minutes, and there were no further sounds from the town up the railroad track. So he clucked to Olney Tyler's horse and the other animals, roped together, were forced to follow the mounted one. He did not hurry and the first shaft of light from the rising sun pointed towards Black Rock as he rode around the corner of the depot building onto Ogden Street.

He saw then why no one had seen him approaching. Every survivor of the gun battle was gathered on the street, silent in mounting grief and diminishing anger after the final act of the horror-filled night. The bodies of Olney Tyler and his eight men were aligned on one side of the street. Those of Mason, Lind, Lodge, Kate Porter, and two other men were laid out on the other side.

The people heard the clop of hooves and all eyes swung towards Steele now. He thought perhaps that in that first instant they saw him, some of them might have been inclined to blast at him. But they had already decided they had had enough of killing and none of them carried a gun now.

Steele rode to within twenty feet of the fringe of the

crowd and halted his horse. He unfastened the rope from his saddlehorn to free the string of horses behind him. The animals remained as still as the people.

'Here's the money South gave them,' Steele said, tossing the sack into the dust between himself and the silent watchers.

Then he unbooted the Colt Hartford and slid from the saddle. He crossed to the body of Gus, which was closest to him, and stooped to turn out the dead man's pockets.

'Robbing the dead?' Hatcher croaked.

'There was eight and a half thousand in their saddlebags,' the Virginian replied without turning from his task. 'I reckon they got some carrying money. It's mine and a widow's in Crest City.'

There was a stir in the crowd and two men pushed to the edge and came clear. Alvin Rhodes and a taller, more distinguished looking man. Steele guessed he was Cedric Harvey, the bank president.

'We owe you a debt of gratitude, sir,' Harvey said as Rhodes scooped up the sack. 'I don't know how you survived and accomplished this – '

'I got a damn good idea!' a man yelled from the centre of the crowd. 'On account of he left this town with no gun nor nothin' of much else. Now look at him!'

Steele completed his chore of searching the dead, rewarded with about five hundred dollars. He moved back to Tyler's horse and swung up into the saddle.

'Well, I as bank president owe you a debt of gratitude, sir!' Harvey insisted. He pointed to the sack Rhodes was holding. 'And not just for this. The railroad is engaged in buying up right of way land to take the track north from Black Rock. There is half a million dollars in the bank vault.'

Steele blinked. 'You've got to be joking, feller,' he rasped.

Harvey grimaced and raked his eyes along the town's dead. 'On a morning like this, sir, I am not moved to be a wit.'

The Virginian nodded. 'Just five hundred thousand?' he mused as he wheeled his horse. 'Just a half-wit I reckon.'

'Steele!' a woman yelled from the crowd. 'You've got blood on your hands in Black Rock. I don't know how, but – '

'Friggin' right!' a recognisable voice cut in. It was Erle, the stage driver. 'We don't need to know friggin' how. You come back this way again and you'll hang, bounty hunter.'

'That's right!' somebody else agreed, and drew a mumble of assent to the warning.

'You're under sentence of death, mister! What they call in the courts one that's . . .

. . . SUSPENDED.'

Like the action until Adam Steele rides a new trail in the next book of the series.

NEL BESTSELLERS

Crime

T013	332	CLOUDS OF WITNESS	*Dorothy L. Sayers* 40p
T016	307	THE UNPLEASANTNESS AT THE BELLONA CLUB	*Dorothy L. Sayers* 40p
T021	548	GAUDY NIGHT	*Dorothy L. Sayers* 40p
T026	698	THE NINE TAILORS	*Dorothy L. Sayers* 50p
T026	671	FIVE RED HERRINGS	*Dorothy L. Sayers* 50p
T015	556	MURDER MUST ADVERTISE	*Dorothy L. Sayers* 40p

Fiction

T018	520	HATTER'S CASTLE	*A. J. Cronin* 75p
T013	944	CRUSADER'S TOMB	*A. J. Cronin* 60p
T013	936	THE JUDAS TREE	*A. J. Cronin* 50p
T015	386	THE NORTHERN LIGHT	*A. J. Cronin* 50p
T026	213	THE CITADEL	*A. J. Cronin* 80p
T027	112	BEYOND THIS PLACE	*A. J. Cronin* 60p
T016	609	KEYS OF THE KINGDOM	*A. J. Cronin* 50p
T027	201	THE STARS LOOK DOWN	*A. J. Cronin* 90p
T018	539	A SONG OF SIXPENCE	*A. J. Cronin* 50p
T001	288	THE TROUBLE WITH LAZY ETHEL	*Ernest K. Gann* 30p
T003	922	IN THE COMPANY OF EAGLES	*Ernest K. Gann* 30p
T023	001	WILDERNESS BOY	*Stephen Harper* 35p
T017	524	MAGGIE D	*Adam Kennedy* 35p
T022	390	A HERO OF OUR TIME	*Mikhail Lermontov* 45p
T025	691	SIR, YOU BASTARD	*G. F. Newman* 40p
T022	536	THE HARRAD EXPERIMENT	*Robert H. Rimmer* 50p
T022	994	THE DREAM MERCHANTS	*Harold Robbins* 95p
T023	303	THE PIRATE	*Harold Robbins* 95p
T022	968	THE CARPETBAGGERS	*Harold Robbins* £1.00
T016	560	WHERE LOVE HAS GONE	*Harold Robbins* 75p
T023	958	THE ADVENTURERS	*Harold Robbins* £1.00
T025	241	THE INHERITORS	*Harold Robbins* 90p
T025	276	STILETTO	*Harold Robbins* 50p
T025	268	NEVER LEAVE ME	*Harold Robbins* 50p
T025	292	NEVER LOVE A STRANGER	*Harold Robbins* 90p
T022	226	A STONE FOR DANNY FISHER	*Harold Robbins* 80p
T025	284	79 PARK AVENUE	*Harold Robbins* 75p
T025	187	THE BETSY	*Harold Robbins* 80p
T020	894	RICH MAN, POOR MAN	*Irwin Shaw* 90p

Historical

T022	196	KNIGHT WITH ARMOUR	*Alfred Duggan* 50p
T022	250	THE LADY FOR RANSOM	*Alfred Duggan* 50p
T015	297	COUNT BOHEMOND	*Alfred Duggan* 50p
T017	958	FOUNDING FATHERS	*Alfred Duggan* 50p
T017	753	WINTER QUARTERS	*Alfred Duggan* 50p
T021	297	FAMILY FAVOURITES	*Alfred Duggan* 50p
T022	625	LEOPARDS AND LILIES	*Alfred Duggan* 60p
T019	624	THE LITTLE EMPERORS	*Alfred Duggan* 50p
T020	126	THREE'S COMPANY	*Alfred Duggan* 50p
T021	300	FOX 10: BOARDERS AWAY	*Adam Hardy* 35p

Science Fiction

T016	900	STRANGER IN A STRANGE LAND	*Robert Heinlein* 75p
T020	797	STAR BEAST	*Robert Heinlein* 35p
T017	451	I WILL FEAR NO EVIL	*Robert Heinlein* 80p
T026	817	THE HEAVEN MAKERS	*Frank Herbert* 35p
T027	279	DUNE	*Frank Herbert* 90p
T022	854	DUNE MESSIAH	*Frank Herbert* 60p
T023	974	THE GREEN BRAIN	*Frank Herbert* 35p
T012	859	QUEST FOR THE FUTURE	*A. E. Van Vogt* 35p
T015	270	THE WEAPON MAKERS	*A. E. Van Vogt* 30p
T023	265	EMPIRE OF THE ATOM	*A. E. Van Vogt* 40p
T017	354	THE FAR-OUT WORLDS OF A. E. VAN VOGT	
			A. E. Van Vogt 40p

NEL BESTSELLERS

NEL P.O. BOX 11, FALMOUTH, CORNWALL

For U.K. and Eire: customers should include to cover postage, 15p for the first book plus 5p per copy for each additional book ordered, up to a maximum charge of 50p.

For Overseas customers and B.F.P.O.: customers should include to cover postage, 20p for the first book and 10p per copy for each additional book.

Name...

Address ....

....

Title ....

(May)